THE SINGING TREE

*to David and Norrie
with appreciation
for your friendship
         Peter*

*Hong Kong
December 1991*

The Singing Tree

PETER MOSS

BLOOMSBURY

All rights reserved: no part of this publication may be reproduced,
stored in a retrieval system, or transmitted in any form or by any
means, electronic, mechanical, photocopying or otherwise, without
the prior written permission of the publisher.

First published 1991
Copyright © 1991 by Peter Moss
The moral right of the author has been asserted

Bloomsbury Publishing Ltd, 2 Soho Square, London W1V 5DE

A CIP catalogue record for this book is available
from the British Library

ISBN 0 7475 0710 4

10 9 8 7 6 5 4 3 2 1

Photoset by Rowland Phototypesetting Ltd
Bury St Edmunds, Suffolk
Printed and bound in Great Britain by
Butler and Tanner Ltd, Frome and London

An ageing rubber planter bides his time in the jungle, awaiting his nemesis. Painfully, secretively, he embarks on his confessions. Mengele was not the last Nazi mass murderer in hiding. He himself, as the youngest station master in Germany, was responsible for the massacre of one hundred and twenty-three innocents in his rail yards – all because he panicked on receiving a hoax phone call that Hitler's express was due at any moment. And he has lived with that guilt ever since.

Children were among those who died that day. Now childless widower Kristian Hardy, alias Kurt Hellmann, delights in the company of a son born to his housekeeper under his roof. Eduardo does not know Kristian is a killer, as they play together in the overgrown music room which can no longer keep out the jungle. The child of Indian blood is captivated by melodies from the Bechstein concert grand improbably brought to this remote place by its former inhabitant – a man whose life Kristian pieces together from letters hidden in the escritoire. Kristian has taken steps to bring about his own retribution, becoming involved in a local Indian vendetta. But into his remote backwater comes Ruth Golding, daughter of Jewish immigrants to New York, who is surely not in Brazil just to hunt for butterflies.

As Kristian Hardy woos his young nemesis, a narrative of resounding beauty and power unfolds. Peter Moss is a craftsman of exquisite subtlety and rich imagination who holds his readers captivated by the stirring harmonies and counterpoints of his prose.

And as they walk, they seem tall pagodas;
And all the ropes let down from the cloud
Ring the hard cold bell-buds upon the trees – codas
Of overtones, ecstasies, grown for love's shroud.

Edith Sitwell, *Façade*

It is living somewhere in the canopy of a rain forest. One of these unknown, inconspicuous insects. No scientist will miss it, except as a statistic.

Martin Holdgate,
Director-General,
World Conservation Union

The world's most intelligent ape is cutting off the branch on which it is sitting.

Andrew W. Mitchell, *The Enchanted Canopy*

FOR KATHLEEN MAUD STAERCK WATSON

PREFACE

I have outlived the length of my own shadow. And am compelled to witness changes mercifully concealed from those sentenced only to their proper spans of life.

The jungle is closing in on me.

Since the last rains the river has found a new channel, looping some half a kilometre further to the east. O Varayo is beginning to perish. Like a gangrenous limb from which a tourniquet has shut off all supply of blood, we are waiting to rot into extinction. For me it cannot come soon enough.

Father Lorenzo is phlegmatic. His faith has convinced him that the river will return. Sometimes, after several centuries, it does. More likely it will steadily push even further east. Faith can be more cruel to the believer than starvation is to the realist. It merely offers a slower way to die.

To admit to the good Father that I welcome the river's desertion would be hardly less difficult than to explain why. How describe my comfort in hearing the ever more muffled shovels of the gravediggers as I am steadily buried alive?

It is time, at last, to lay down my burden on paper, to record what hitherto I have not dared reveal of my reasons for being here.

Even illiterate murderers on Death Row fulfil their desire to scratch on the walls the pitiful graffiti of their passing through this life. My cell is so remote that, when my time comes to leave, it may never be discovered. And if it is, like some buried Inca tomb, it will surrender nothing of its secrets but the rotted, illegible pages of this journal on which I now embark.

Only the piano, I hope, will confound them.

For God knows I have loved it, and tended it, as the only remnant of a life from which I derive no other pride.

When they hack through the vines and clear the rubble from the doorway it will be standing here, its beautiful black top rearing up in the sunlight like the wing of a giant butterfly.

And when the boldest among them advances to lift the lid and plant his fingers on the dusty keys, a chord will be released like the liberated sigh of a last painful memory, ringing through the forest and raising the macaws.

My reverie ends there, with my final enigmatic message carrying through the trees in a minor key and the piano, having waited to deliver it, falling silent at last through the depredations of the termites and the wood wasps.

But the chances are that, having quickly recovered from their surprise, the visitors will gather round and hammer out the latest violations of pop music imported from the coast.

And dance upon my grave.

For this is Brazil!

Well, let them.

My spirit will be dancing with them.

I have just had a striking illustration of how far this little world is divorced from the mechanisms that propel the rest of the planet. Only yesterday, a two-year-old copy of *Newsweek* drifted into my backwater, bearing news of Josef Mengele. They claim to have dug up his remains down in Embu, thus ending 'the greatest manhunt in history'.

If it is true, Mengele must have spent some six years laughing in his grave, because those who buried him claim he drowned at least that much earlier on the beach at Bertioga. A merciful death for the man known as the Angel of Death and the Butcher of Auschwitz. That great Jewish Avenger, Simon Wiesenthal, described him as 'the last living mass murderer from Hitler's and Himmler's death factories'.

The reward money totalled $3.4 million!

Beside him, poor old Adolf Eichmann pales into insignificance. And they never even allowed Adolf a grave to rest in. His judges in Jerusalem made sure of that!

But they are wrong about Mengele. He is not the last Nazi mass murderer. I am here as the living proof.

PASTORALE

I

When we first came here the house was still visible from the river, partly obscured by trees but retaining, from a distance, something of the effect its builder had striven to create.

It was the only structure for several hundred kilometres made of brick and stone. Not quite the megalomaniac achievement that gave Manáus its opera house, but strange and exotic enough to awe the natives.

It was not what I was looking for, or had expected to find. I needed something much less conspicuous for my refuge.

But the piano – a Bechstein concert grand – captured and held me.

Unable either to leave it here, or take it with me, I had no option but to stay and rebuild my life around it.

I could learn little of the previous occupant. Why he chose to live in such style, and what use, if any, he made of the Bechstein. It had been some six years since he disappeared without a trace.

Ironically, he was known to his peons as the Station Master, a planter who had bought into an estate co-operative and had been allocated this particular station to manage, covering a tract of about a hundred hectares. Some said he left to enlist in the war. But since it was not their war they could not say why, or on whose side. Others claimed he was killed by his Indian wife, who had also disappeared, to avenge the decimation of her tribe by the inroads of planters like him.

He was not remembered as a cruel man. In fact he was barely

remembered at all, so quickly does the jungle erase the meagre traces of our struggles against it.

This is the last wilderness. Elsewhere on this continent the struggle is almost over. Man has conquered, only to be conquered in return by the slow erosion of all those conditions necessary to sustain his life. We have become our own cancer, eating deeper into these green lungs which first breathed life into us. When we have finally slashed and burned our way through the last of the forest, when the rain no longer falls and the desert spreads across the bold new worlds we have so impatiently forged, the vanished trees will exact their own posthumous revenge.

I like that word in this context. Posthumous. Post-humus.

Like the vengeful Indian wife, the dead forest will poison its murderers.

But I stray from my point. The house. And its enigmatic owner.

Whatever the truth behind their mystery, the perception was highly unfavourable. The superstitious Indians and the hardly less superstitious *seringueíros* who worked the plantation believed the building to be haunted. They carved up and fought over the land, but they left the house alone.

The Bechstein stood silent, in a room turning green with the mildew on the walls and the thrusting forays of vegetation through the windows, until the day I pushed open the doors and stood enraptured at the sight of it.

I endeavoured to acquire the property through legal process, only to learn that, whether or not it had claimed the owner, the war had brought bankruptcy and dissolution to the co-operative. My lawyer in Rio confessed himself unable to trace the title. The house and the land were up for grabs, and the land had long been taken.

We had no choice but to become squatters. And our rights were uncontested by our squatter neighbours, who watched with interest as we moved in, convinced we would not long survive the disturbance of whatever malevolent spirits might reside here.

It was difficult, at first, to hire their assistance in repairing the damage and making the place habitable, but fortunately I had both time and money on my side. And the good sense not to play the arrogant intruder with a disposition to order them about.

They came to accept that I was not here to seize their lands back from them in the name of the former owners. They were even willing to consider selling to me what they had taken without authority. And they found I was ready to pay a fair price.

Some stayed on to work the land for me. They were, after all, poor settlers who had succumbed to their government's propaganda to move west and had reaped, for their pains, malaria, disillusionment and meagre returns. The estate had been broken up into smallholdings, improperly managed and unscientifically cultivated.

I set out to show them what could be achieved with a fuller understanding of rubber and the conditions required for its extraction in a way that would not needlessly damage and shorten the lifespan of the trees.

What I taught myself of the subject was gleaned from books published in Britain, documenting the findings of those who, many years ago, had smuggled its seeds from Brazil and, with the horticultural wizardry of Kew Gardens, had turned rubber into one of the world's most widely planted and profitable crops, extending throughout the eastern archipelagos.

The books were already here, some of them bonded together through years of humidity. Salvaging them became as much a work of art as a labour of love, to which I devoted the patient attention a museum curator might lavish on a threatened masterpiece.

There was little else in the way of literature, and, again, much of that was in English rather than Portuguese, increasing my curiosity as to the identity and interests of my predecessor. Scattered in untidy confusion throughout the rooms were a few volumes on estate management and labour legislation, and what I assumed to be the entire collected works of Conan Doyle.

We had brought almost nothing with us but the scrip I had redeemed, when the time came, from my bankers in Rio. Faced with the task of keeping my mind from decaying faster than the books, I improved upon my knowledge of English, acquired in my youth as part of my training for coping with the tourist traffic passing through the German rail network in the thirties. And I set to work restoring these miscellaneous volumes to as much legibility as the ravages of time would allow.

It suited my purpose to do so, for I had already embarked on cultivating a new persona, needing to distance myself from my native tongue.

In the course of which I mastered three attributes in which I take pride: the skill to piece together, despite innumerable missing pages, the profiles of the killers Sherlock Holmes endeavoured to unmask; my talents as a piano tuner; and, as I say, a proper understanding of the rubber business. Mine became the best managed plantation in the upper Amazon basin, and the only one to be restored as a fully operational estate, processing its own sheet and shipping downstream direct to the major ports.

By avoiding the middle men, I made a fortune in the boom days up to and including the Korean War, and held my own even in the difficult years when synthetic substitutes were beginning to take the edge off the industry.

I paid my *seringueiros* well and kept their loyalty. I have seen two generations tap my trees, and the survivors are with me still.

Survivors is the word. For rubber is no longer the force it was, and the government's policy of opening up the hinterland to decant the overflow from the work-hungry coastal populations has swept up the youth of this tiny backwater with the promise of greater riches from tin and gold in the newly discovered alluvial deposits to the south.

El Dorado fever is still as endemic in the blood of this country as the ineradicable scourge of malaria. And now that the river too is deserting us, the task of extracting and shipping the rubber becomes more difficult and less economic.

Just as I myself become more lethargic and less interested. Though still fit and able, I have reached the point now where I am disinclined to ride, or even walk about the estate as I used to. So that I no longer check on the efficiency of my overseers. With each rainy season the roads fall further into neglect, cutting off more and more tracts of land where the trees are now too old to yield and where the expense of replacing them seems hardly justified.

We are falling into stagnation, the land and I, succumbing to the terrible resignation and apathy that begins, nerve by nerve, to cauterise the senses of the steadily more senile.

I am seventy-two years old. And I have no heir to pick up the reins when they will fall from my insensible fingers.

I was once the youngest station master in Germany.

I am now surely the oldest station master in Brazil.

2

When we planned the reconstruction of the house, which I should more correctly describe as a mansion, we deliberately left this rear annex untouched. We didn't need the space. The rest of the building was ample for our requirements. And it was not, in any case, structurally essential to the main wing, having apparently been added as an afterthought.

But I didn't pull it down either, for I liked the anarchy of vegetation which had taken root here, and which has since escalated to the extent that house and forest are inseparably entwined.

If the flooring were not so unreliable I would dearly love to move the Bechstein and turn this former guest suite into a proper music room.

I like the ever changing play of light here, the way in which the movement of the leaves, reaching delicate fingers into the entrails of this man-made edifice, reflects the viridescent depths of the forest. The house seems at times a vessel that has suffered a mortal wound in its struggle with the sea, and is now sinking into an ever darker, ever greener embrace, as cool and as calming as death itself.

Sometimes I tread warily across the sagging timbers to feel the texture of the foliage, allowing it to brush across my face like the touch of a blind man.

'Here I am,' I whisper. 'Stroke me, embrace me. Soon I too will be yours.'

The longer I have lived here the more I have come to realise that the simple animism of primitive man is closer to God than anything our intellect has devised, with all its ecstasy and ritual.

Even without the Bechstein, it is a room filled with music. Indeed I think of it as my music room. For the one other inheritance left me by my mysterious benefactor is a little treasure trove of piano scores, with a leaning to the French composers: Ravel, Debussy, Fauré and even Poulenc. The room can be all of these, shifting moods as swiftly as a breeze or with the stately solemnity of cloud armadas sailing across the sun.

Mostly it is Debussy, with all the richness of tone and nuance of shading he could derive from a single colour. Aquamarine.

I am almost never reminded of Beethoven or Brahms. But occasionally the room will resonate with a dimly remembered phrase of Schubert or an entire sonata of Mozart. Only then am I ungrateful enough to regret that whoever assembled these scores omitted the Germanic composers.

I could, of course, write to Boosey & Hawkes for their catalogues, but my reluctance to be included on anyone's mailing lists, even under my assumed name, is still there.

3

With the ticking seconds settling like motes of dust into the undisturbed nooks and crannies of my ever more sedentary life, I find I am spending more and more time in the music room. I sit by the escritoire in the only corner still safe to inhabit, fingering my scores, re-reading Doyle or a tattered back number of *Newsweek* that has found its way upriver aboard the trading boats. Or simply allowing my mind to interlock with the web of greenery enmeshing the room and tapping into my thoughts.

I can pass a whole afternoon watching the sinking sun raise its tide-marks of shadow upon the lichened walls. Or waiting for the fine dribble of powder that presages the fall of another peeling stalactite of plaster from the ceiling. For the leaves caress my senses like the strings of a harp.

When all light and colour has finally drained from the room, and Esquamillo has prodded into life the generator that powers the main wing of the house, I return there, to seat myself at the Bechstein and extract from the keyboard echoes of the music I have accumulated through the afternoon.

The fame of this instrument has spread through the forest. Occasionally a migrant tribe of Indians will stop by and request a performance, having heard of the precedent set when I volunteered to entertain a party of monkey hunters with the 'Golliwogg's Cakewalk'. Either my playing is so inept as to fail entirely to capture the humour of the piece or the novelty of the experience constrains them to a dignified solemnity verging on reverence. Neither at my début, nor since, have I managed to extract the merest hint of a smile.

Wide-eyed wonder, yes, but not amusement. And the wonder increases with the intensity of the piece. I wish Debussy were here to see the expressions produced on the faces of these naked innocents by his *Sunken Cathedral*. Or Ravel to watch the effect as, enclosed in a thicket of bows and blowpipes, I have them almost imperceptibly swaying to his *Valse*.

It is not that they lack exposure to music. Some of them trek through the jungle with the earphones of their battered and bartered Walkmans drowning out the birds. But they have come to accept the sound as something manufactured, divorced from human artistry. They perceive it, if they have stopped to consider it at all, as a product encoded in the delicate moving parts of their intricate mechanisms, which, if they cease to function and cannot be revived by a change of batteries, must be abandoned on the march.

To hear music coaxed by human hand from a beautifully carved piece of furniture is as wondrous an experience for them as the first phonograph must have seemed to my grandfather.

My strangest musical memory is of a touring ballet group, improbably and inexplicably engaged by one of the larger mining companies to enliven the tedium of its workers encamped upstream, who found themselves stranded in our midst by exceptional rains that made the river unnavigable.

Learning from Father Lorenzo of the existence of my piano, they had themselves ferried along the flooded channel to my estate and accepted the hospitality I had no recourse but to extend.

For three days they camped in whatever shelter my roof could offer, while Esquamillo and Estancia surrendered the kitchen to them for the meals they cooked in relays and suffered the pennants of their laundry to proliferate in sodden festivity down the lengths of corridor.

They were a lively bunch, seething with energy and impatient to be off. Instead of resigning themselves to the imprisoning rain, they gathered around the Bechstein to go through their repertoire again and again, as if rehearsing for a royal command performance rather than an audience of miners.

Their particular concern was to perfect the choreography of a new work by a Russian composer, based on Bizet's *Carmen*. I was assured that the scoring was for strings and percussion only. Which I would have thought rendered all the more unsatisfactory the substitution of a mere piano. But their director seemed content that this would at least supply the melodic outline.

He was anxious that the tunes themselves, and not the mere rhythms, should govern the shape of the dance.

He would interrupt the routines, hammering on the keyboard with both fists and yelling, 'Forget the tempo. Listen to the music. Sing it with your feet. Sing it with your hands. Don't just dance it.'

Estancia was as mystified as those of her fellow Indians who happened to be sheltering from the rain in the further reaches of the mansion. Standing with them in the doorway, her prim, freshly laundered smock in sharp contrast to their glistening thighs and torsos, she stared wide-eyed as Carmen performed a slow, explicit *pas de deux* with Escamillo the matador.

The eroticism was too much for her own Esquamillo, who covered his wife's eyes with a napkin and led her back to the kitchen.

When the generator, and my inadequate lighting, failed to compensate for the gathering darkness, the two of them brought in candles and hurricane lamps which the dancers distributed about the hallway with the mock ceremony of celebrants at a mass. This impromptu ritual was sheer magic to the Indians, one of whom made the sign of the cross and went down on his knees.

4

It is difficult for me to judge how far the Indians trust me. No more so, perhaps, than for them to *decide* how far they can trust me. They have seen so much betrayal that they have all but lost their innocence. And now they avoid eye contact, even when addressing me, for fear of losing more.

These are not the real bush Indians but the marginals; the ones who are two steps out of Eden and three steps into hell. Their faces tell it, hardened to the perfidies they have come to expect in their dealings with both *sertanéjos* and *seringueíros*, although of the two they will still rather have the former than the latter.

Ours, according to reports of the Indian experts at FUNAI, is one of the quieter areas, where the worst of the culture clash is over and the beginnings of an accommodation have been reached. In neighbouring territories, where the cutting edge of land 'development' is still carving into what remains of the virgin forest, the *seringueíros* carry their guns with them at all times, ready to kill or be killed. The Indians have too many old scores to settle.

Father Lorenzo contends the only way we can save the tribes is to enforce a massive withdrawal of all the settlers, the planters, the miners, the farmers and the foresters, removing everything we ever brought with us and leaving the forest to heal its scars.

'Taking even our God?' I asked.

'Even our God,' he whispered, and I knew the agonising that must have led him to that conclusion. He thinks of himself not as a missionary but as a doctor priest. One who is here to relieve the distress, both physical and spiritual, suffered on this battlefront between God and Pan.

He is the scion of one of the country's oldest families; pure-blooded Portuguese who have been here more than two hundred years, making their fortune from exploitation of every possible resource, animal, vegetable, mineral and human. His forebears hunted Indians for slaves and, when they tired of that, hunted them for sport. He came here, I know, to expiate their sins. And though he sounds now as if he is ready to concede defeat, claiming the task is too great and his gesture too infinitesimal, I know too that he cannot leave. Like me, he has the jungle vines locked about his heart.

'Whatever I do or say, they see me as just another invader,' he complains. 'One who is less arrogant and insensitive than the others, perhaps. But one who is nevertheless here, like the rest, to steal from them. Only what I would take is most valuable of all, for it is nothing less than their souls.'

I tell him that, if we leave now, every one of us, taking with us every trace of our presence here, including our totem God, it is too late. The natives are already infected with our fatal disease. They may hate us for it, but we have made them dependent upon us. They are like wild dogs that have known the comfort of a camp fire and are driven to follow at heel when the hunters strike their tents.

Even if it were possible to restore it to them, whole and complete as it once was, their world will never again be enough for them.

The book of Doyle's I have enjoyed most is his *Lost World*, an impossible odyssey in which Professor Challenger discovers, somewhere on this continent, a plateau left undisturbed since that 'dawn of time' so beloved of the English romantics. However brief his presence among them, it was enough to ensure that those primitives who had lived in ignorance of the wider world would now be lost to their own. And that, to me, was the real significance of the book's title.

Which is why, when the boy Eduardo was born to Esquamillo, who is half Indian, and Estancia, who is fully so, I wished the child could be sent instantly into the forest, to be raised by his mother's tribe, and not open his eyes to the world that has seduced his parents. But it was impossible, of course, to explain this to the devoted pair who had served me so long and who, after losing so many in infancy, saw themselves blessed this late in their years by one last hope of posterity.

Thus, through the futility of my doing anything to prevent it, I have watched the child become ever more inextricably entangled in my life, like the tiny creatures inhabiting the foliage of the music room, unaware of the barrier they crossed when they ventured beyond the shattered window.

And now he too is securely wrapped around my heart.

KINDERSCENEN

I

The music room is our favourite retreat. But I have yet to teach him that we can only sit and watch from the escritoire. Now that he can walk, and his little legs carry him everywhere, he is liable to get up and leave my side before I can stop him.

He did so just yesterday, turning me cold with fear. I had reached over to collect a fallen leaf which I could explain to him when suddenly he tottered out across the floor to fetch another.

I have never properly tested the flooring, although I have ventured out across it myself to those spots I know to be safe. But other than the environs of the desk, and that area where I come into contact with the tree, the rest is unknown and potentially hazardous territory.

For years I have watched the brass bed that once stood against the far wall listing steadily to port and settling into the timbers like a waterlogged raft doomed eventually to sink beneath the waves. It was towards this that Eduardo confidently headed.

Without stopping to think, I ran after him, scooping him up in my arms and dashing back to the safety of the escritoire. I seemed to hear, even as I did so, the whole room cry out in alarm, and then settle to the plaintive creaking of a tired old ship disturbed by a freak swell on an otherwise calm sea.

Eduardo laughed and struggled to escape from my grasp, thinking it a game. I was driven in my anxiety to scold him, for the first time, and the surprise of it brimmed in his dark, liquid eyes.

I cannot look into those eyes without feeling as vulnerable

myself as they make him appear. They are eyes that have seen no betrayal and can yet conceive of its possibility. Eyes that gaze already beyond the realms of innocence to the journey into wisdom. Eyes that must learn, as time goes by, what to shut out and what to keep in.

As yet they are windows open to the world, through which I can look once more upon what was lost to me so very long ago.

I had not wanted the boy enthralled by my world, but I see now that I am more his captive than he can ever be mine.

After being left so long a childless widower, I am completely unprepared for what I now experience, the tenderness and protectiveness that well up in me at the sight of him, feelings of which I had thought myself incapable.

How many children have passed through my hands? Hundreds? Thousands? And I trained myself never to look into their faces. I was just doing my job. They were items on a list of movement orders, no more. In transit from their various origins to a station down the line. And I had merely to throw the lever and set the points to put them on the right track.

Most were further distanced from me by their parents, with whom they travelled in family units, carefully labelled and docketed with numbers and identification tabs.

I must stop writing. Something very disturbing occurred just a moment ago when Estancia came to take her son from me and put him to bed. I could not bring myself to part with him.

Estancia assumed I was merely being playfully avuncular. She thinks, with good reason, that I spoil him, and I had to let it pass for that.

But the pain of it, creeping up on me so unexpectedly, has left me trembling. And, anyway, the light is draining from the room so that I can no longer see the words.

2

The house is set upon a rise so that, from my bedroom, I look across a sea of rubber stretching to the margins of the forest.

Beyond that transition into darker shades of green roll the wider, deeper oceans of verdure as yet unplumbed by extractors of minerals and timber.

Out on those uncharted wastes break the storms that give these forests their name, releasing the rains that either benignly endow them with life or devastatingly wash that life away.

We observe the building of the storms, Eduardo and I. The towering thunderclouds erupting above the cumulus to flatten their ugly anvil heads high above the plains and rend the air with their lightning.

Eduardo loves them. I have taught him that there is nothing to fear in them. That the storms are a necessary purging of our stagnant afternoons to usher in the cleansing showers of evening.

Most exciting of all is to watch the coming of the wind that precedes the rain. We follow its movement as it approaches across the forest like a giant tsunami, crashing through the waves of treetop and sucking up loose leaves and branches in its path.

Bearing him in my arms, I race through the house to the door of the music room, just in time to see the wind grip and shake the branch of our tree, making it writhe as if it were charged with a million volts of electricity. With any luck its arrival will coincide with a thunderbolt that drenches the room in light and deafens our ears, causing Eduardo to hug me in a mixture of terror and exultation.

I do not want him to be afraid of anything except his conscience. And pray God he will never have reason to fear that.

3

His parents show no sign of begrudging me the time I spend with the boy. Indeed it pleases them that their son pleases me. And I discipline myself not to monopolise him. After my unaccountable reluctance that night to return him to Estancia, I force myself to lead him back to her before it becomes necessary for her to come and fetch him.

And so far he seems equally happy to be with all three of us, knowing he can count on an equal share of love from each.

In that sense I have become – and they have tacitly allowed me to become – a third, albeit surrogate, parent. With Eduardo making no distinctions between us except that one is mother, another is father and the third is known to him as uncle.

Each of us, of course, has a different role. Estancia equals food, bath, bed and discipline. Esquamillo represents outdoor adventure and alfresco discoveries of what a hunter and a fisherman can provide. For the man still insists on supplementing our meals with the trophies of the forest and of the narrow, clogged-up stream that barely connects us with the distant river. And I envy him his younger, sturdier body.

I provide the boy with games and stories and the stuff that will flex and expand his imagination.

Also I play music for him. Parts of Schumann's *Kinderscenen* from memory and, repeatedly, all of Debussy's *Children's Corner* with special encores of the 'Golliwogg's Cakewalk'.

We are well beyond the reach of television, and I will not allow even a radio in the house. All that penetrate this far are the faintest tremors of a world that is threshing like a blind, deranged giant far below the horizon. We get what the Americans call scattered fragments of the fall-out, and my view of their source is narrowed to the strangely compressed and distorted telescope of news magazines that arrive in random order weeks, sometimes months, old. Reading them, I am struck sometimes by the thought that I am leafing through the notebooks of naturalists observing the behaviour of some curious species of animal.

The reports are so cold, so clinical, so matter of fact.

It is difficult to know what to impart to the child when my own education is now falling so far behind. It is tempting to teach him nothing, to assume that the giant will never rear its terrible form above our horizon. But that is a vain hope.

I listen for its footsteps, knowing that if it draws much nearer the tsunami that precedes it will tear to shreds the microcosm I have created for myself. Only I know what that wind can do, for once already it has blown my world apart.

Despite my efforts to discourage him, Esquamillo occasionally addresses me as Station Master. I can't blame him. It was the name they gave my predecessor in this house and he has no idea of the connotations it holds for me.

I was the youngest station master in Germany. The appointment made me a celebrity in our community. The local newspaper hailed it with pride, even though the station I managed was among the smallest in the country.

Not too small to escape the changes brought about by the war, when my branch line carried some of the heaviest traffic on the system.

Of all the memories I try to suppress, the most persistent is the voice on the phone. I recall precisely the accent, the severity of the tone, the exact words of the message it delivered, giving me notice of the fact that the Führer was on his way to visit the troops and that his express train was due any minute.

'I want no excuses,' the voice barked. 'I don't care who or what is on it. Clear the line. You hear me? Clear the line!'

I was the youngest station master in Germany.

I cleared the line.

Of seven hundred and forty-two men, women and children just disembarked to board the cattle cars awaiting them in the siding. Six hundred and nineteen of them survived the stampede across the rails as they were driven before the rifle butts of their guards.

In response to instructions I received from an unidentified voice on the telephone.

I had not stopped to consider that there were no troops stationed on that line worthy of a visit by the Führer. That this was the last corner of the country he would be concerned with at this point of the war. I just did what I was told.

It was a joke. One hundred and twenty-three people died for a joke.

Played on the youngest station master in Germany.

The youngest.

It is too late for me to edit my life, omitting what I do not care to remember and what I could not stand to witness again. I did what I did. There is no one I can blame for that.

Youth. Obedience to orders. The discipline of the service. There is no excuse to be found in any of that.

I did what I did.

But I am in a position here to edit the world of another while it is still in the process of formation.

I look at Eduardo and I think how unbearable it is that he should be exposed to the things I have seen.

And the world is rotten with it. Still rotten with it, and getting worse.

What more proof is needed when it is there to read in the news magazines, the evidence of it piling up day by day, hour by hour?

No. I will not let that happen here.

I have the power to save one life from the fire. I control this world. There is still music here, the light playing on the leaves, the movement of tiny living things in the branches. And the primal power of nature, with its cleansing winds and rains.

It is just a matter of deciding what to teach him.

And what to leave out.

4

I will have to watch my step.

The time will come when he will outpace me and I can no longer keep up. Already he wears me out with his demands for piggy-back rides. I am getting too old to be carrying him up and down the stairs, and if I fall I dread to think of the consequences.

This morning I tripped on the hall carpet, unable to save myself from crashing down with him underneath me.

I panicked.

He just lay there on his back, staring up at me.

It was just a fraction of a second, and it was just surprise on his part because he wasn't sure if we were perhaps playing another game.

Yet I distinctly heard the ugly bump as his head hit the floor, confirmed when my fingers found the swelling beneath his scalp.

He laughed. He decided it *was* a game.

It must be the Indian in him. Implanted in his genes. The ability to suffer pain in silence.

Many jungle creatures possess it. Not to cry out when the arrow strikes blindly through the thicket can mean all the difference between discovery and survival. Only when death is inevitable can the victim afford the luxury of one final despairing scream.

All the more reason for care. I cannot risk hurting him without knowing I have done so.

He is still too young to sense the difference between us, except in regard to size. He does not know what age is. What age can do.

And suddenly – quite suddenly – I find that, after all, I *do* want to live. That I have a reason to live.

He has given me, for the first time in more than half my life, a purpose for enduring other than to maintain the Bechstein and keep it in tune.

I do it now for him, as is the case with everything I do. My life revolves around him, and I only hope there is enough of it left.

The Bechstein is becoming increasingly difficult to preserve. The wood is still sound, bearing up amazingly well, but the humidity has taken its toll and some of the wire is now rusted beyond recovery. My mechanical ingenuity has so far stood me in good stead, but where am I going to find new wire of the same thickness that will deliver anything approximating the correct tone?

Until I can, I am trying to adapt by confining myself to pieces that omit those particular notes.

But he has noticed. I am sure he has noticed. Inevitably there are some pieces he has become used to hearing in full, and when a note is missing, however marginal it may be, he senses it immediately. I am absolutely certain of it.

Sitting in my lap to listen and watch, he will spot the omission and twist his head to look up at me quizzically.

He has such an acute sense of hearing.

At first he tried imitating me, his little fingers reaching out to push the keys. But when he found this resulted only in discord he pulled back as if from the effects of an electric shock.

And now, despite my encouragement to join in, he is prepared only to watch where I place my hands. Foolish as it may seem, I am convinced he has an acute ear for music. Perhaps even perfect pitch.

Is it conceivable that he will become the first full-blooded Indian concert pianist in the history of music?

God forbid that he become a rock musician.

Rather that I should destroy the Bechstein now.

Not because of their music but because of the life they lead.

Even a concert pianist must go on tour. And be exposed to that world beyond the footlights.

And yet how terrible, if he has that potential, to deny it to the world.

What world?

What is there left out there that is worthy of him?

THRENODY

I

A party of my tappers came for me this morning and urged me to accompany them to an area of the plantation where the trees have long been abandoned and where I have allowed them to establish smallholdings for their crops of cacao and brazil nut. I thought at first they needed me to settle some dispute over boundaries.

I had Eduardo with me, who would not be left behind, so I carried him on my shoulder until one of the *seringueiros* relieved me of his weight.

I wish they had warned me what we would find.

They had been digging a drainage ditch along the margins of their clearance, at a point where the old trees were still succumbing to their chainsaws.

And the shovels had dug into flesh.

I was angry when I saw what they had uncovered. Thinking only of Eduardo, I turned and wrenched him from the arms of the startled *seringueiro*, burying the boy's face against my chest.

'Why didn't you tell me?' I shouted. 'Why did you let me bring the boy?'

It was a stupid, insensitive reaction, of course, and later, when I had calmed down, I apologised.

For a child had died there. A child barely nine years older than Eduardo, so recently that the skin remained intact, except for the cut made by the spade and an ugly gash across her neck, where a razor had taken her life.

She was an Indian girl, and I sensed immediately what that must mean.

Even here we are not spared such brutalities.

She would have been kidnapped from her tribe to cater to the appetite of some trespasser into the Indian reserve. In this part of the country, where the women are never enough to go around, such abductions are common. Possibly the girl was too young, too frightened, too obstinate to co-operate. And her kidnapper would have been unwilling to retrace their path and return her to her tribe, from whom he would know what to expect.

But why had she been brought here?

'Who did this?' I demanded, expecting my question to be greeted with silence.

But they were frightened. The body had been found on their land and already one of the diggers, a halfbreed hired from the wharf at O Varayo, was on his way to report the death to the tribe, where his loyalties still lay.

The *seringueiros* wanted my protection, and they were willing to reveal the identity of the suspect so as to deflect the blame from themselves. The man they fingered was himself a tapper, whom they had never liked and who had left without explanation only yesterday.

They thought he had run away to avoid paying his gambling debts, but now they were convinced he had killed and buried the girl here from spite, knowing the body would quickly be discovered and hoping they would be accused of the crime.

There was nothing for it but to wait for the Indians to arrive. Matters like this require delicate negotiation.

But I couldn't permit Eduardo to remain. He had seen too much already.

I ordered the tapper who had carried him to bear him back to the house.

The man seemed relieved to have a reason for absenting himself.

There were fourteen tribals in the party, outnumbering us two to one, all of them daubed with hunting paint and armed with spears and bows. I could see from their faces that, unlike me, they had been forewarned of what to expect.

Most were familiar to me, having been on my estate several times, some of them gathering around the piano to hear the wonders of the music-making machine. But if they recognised me they gave no sign of it.

While they were covering the last few paces towards us I stepped forward to meet them, holding out my hands to show we carried no weapons.

'We have sent for you . . . ' I began, picking with care the few words of their language I knew which would carry the gist of what I must cautiously impart.

But I was impatiently brushed aside as their leader continued past me to the edge of the uncovered grave.

He stood there with bowed head while the others gathered around him.

They had brought with them a woman who, I assumed, was the mother of the dead girl. It was she who broke their silence and, even though I was braced for it, her cry went through me like a knife.

It was a cry I had heard too often, and had forced myself to ignore, in the days when such pain was an everyday occurrence I had to contend with in carrying out my work.

Heard here, in isolation, in this remote jungle clearing on the edge of the world, it rang through my memory to evoke all of the agony against which I had ever turned my back.

Had it not been necessary, once again, to outface their anger, her raw scream would have brought me to my knees. I am now too old to endure such pain with composure. All my defences have long been worn down.

But I had to remain calm and in command in order to negotiate, possibly for the lives of all of us.

It was a long, patient business.

I saw no point in concealing the fact that we had a suspect. I even gave them his name. But this was not enough, of course. They wanted him handed over to them.

Useless to protest to such people that the law must take its course.

What law?

Whose law?

And who would come to enforce it?

They have heard such promises before, and too seldom seen them kept.

Their chief made it clear that they held me personally responsible. I must deliver the killer to them or pay the forfeit.

It was absurd of course, and I should have treated it with scorn. But, wearying of the parley, I suddenly heard myself, as would a detached observer, consenting to that impossible demand. I listened to myself responding in words my mind had not quite formed, accepting their terms on condition only that I be given ample time to track down the suspect.

I expressed it clumsily. The Indians have little concept of time. The moon is their only calendar. I said that if, by the birth of the thirteenth moon, I had not found and delivered the girl's killer, I would come alone to their village without waiting for them to fetch me.

My words were greeted with silence. Shock on the part of the *seringueiros* and suspicion on the part of the Indians, who probably thought I was bluffing.

But courtesy demanded they must accept my pledge at face value. Honour had been served. It was enough to bring the negotiations to an acceptable conclusion.

Escorting me back to the house, the tappers chorused their concern on my behalf. They volunteered to form posses to track down the killer and bring him back so that I could hand him over to the justice of the tribe.

I said no, I could not afford to lose their help on the estate, where labour is already scarce. If they heard of the whereabouts of the man, and it were possible to apprehend him without days of wasted effort, I would agree to such a search party, but not otherwise.

I was not being brave. Just practical. The chances of finding him now are negligible. This country is the world's greatest labyrinth and he will have no reason to return to the scene of the crime.

Only when Eduardo tottered forward to meet me at the door did I allow myself to absorb the full significance of what I have done.

As recently as a year ago I would have welcomed such an opportunity, embracing it as a merciful respite after years of waiting. What better way to atone for the past than to accept the penalty for a crime I did *not* commit, imposed by a people I have done nothing to offend?

It is enough to make me believe in a patient and merciful God who, in good time, finds ways to grant all prayers.

But now there is Eduardo. And I have discovered work to do that I must leave unfinished.

So be it. At least he will be spared the disillusionment of watching me grow older still.

2

The music room is silent tonight. Eduardo is in bed as I remain here at the escritoire with a candle to light the pages of my journal.

No music comes to me.

No music at all.

The leaves do not stir. There is no colour left in them. They stand stiff as a palisade between me and the creeping, cringing shadows they cast on the far wall. They have lost their tunes. Or else I have lost my ear for their muted voices.

This house is getting old.

If I leave it to Esquamillo, will they stay here? Will they keep the boy with them, letting him run free in his domain?

I like to think of him growing up in this room. Of the room lasting long enough to bear the weight of his maturing mind, nourishing him with the music it has played for me.

He is learning already, I think, to hear those tunes.

He smiles with satisfaction at the subtle progressions of the light, sharing my pleasure in that wonderful *son et lumière* that carries us from morning through afternoon and into evening.

There are times when this room is a cathedral, an aviary, a greenhouse, a diving bell submerged in an oceanic trench. Even the mysterious heart of a living, breathing engine that drives the planet. And we have long sensed, he and I, that if we could only reach in safety the window through which the forest comes to greet us, we will find ourselves on the edge of a secret sea that no one else has ever discovered.

Even without him, I would like, before I die, to squeeze myself through the tangle of branches and see if we have guessed right.

Estancia comes with a candle in one hand and my supper tray in the other. She knows I have seldom stayed here this late, but she has brought my meal to me without asking because she has heard what happened today in the clearing. She says nothing. She does not need to. Her eyes say it.

We understand each other, Estancia and I. In a way that reinforces my faith in the fundamental telepathic power all people possess if only they know how to use it. The primitives have it. They have never lost it. Seeking explanations for it is like asking a dog why it reacts to a sound pitched beyond our hearing.

But this is just one of her many qualities that defy description. She is a creature rooted in the forest yet entangled with the Church. Perhaps her quiet sublimity springs from the fact that she was delivered prematurely, in mid-Mass, beneath the fourth Station of the Cross, where Jesus encountered his mother. Her miraculous survival caused the priest, Father Lorenzo's predecessor, to name her Estancia as a cross between *estaçãó* (station) and *esperança* (hope).

She is my silent familiar. With Esquamillo I must fall back on conversation, but his wife and I communicate without need of speech.

What she conveys to me tonight is her inexpressible sadness for what I have done. But she will not try to dissuade me from the course upon which I am set because she is Indian and she knows too what the tribe has suffered.

Estancia belongs to the tribe diminished today by the meaningless loss of that child. It could have been her child. Aware of how much I love Eduardo, she understands why I must offer atonement. It is the honourable thing to do. And if the Indians have nothing else left to them, they have their honour.

Her acceptance is my benediction. More soothing than any absolution I might be granted in a confessional by a stranger in clerical raiment whose face remains hidden from me.

If only it were possible to do so, I would confide everything to her here and now. I crave that relief. To have just one fellow being perceive the full extent of my guilt.

I have read somewhere that the Incas selected for sacrifice could choose as their executioners the ones they loved the most. Knowing that the blade which cut the heart from them would be swift and merciful?

God grant Estancia will intercede with her tribe to end it cleanly.

I will lay down this journal now and go to bed, strangely at peace with myself for the first time in years.

No wonder this room has not delivered its music today. So radically has my life altered, in the passage from dawn to sunset, that for once I am not in tune with it.

CAPRICCIO

I

I had an appointment today with the agent who handles my sales. We meet once a year to renegotiate the contracts, and because time is more pressing for him than it is for me, these meetings usually take place in our favourite saloon on the waterfront rather than at the house.

His name is Alberto Da Cruz. He started handling my affairs just after the boom years when the markets became more difficult and it was once again necessary to depend upon those who had the contacts and the best access to customers.

I have found him generally reliable and reasonably honest about the deals he arranges on my behalf.

He has heard of my pact with the Indians. Along the river, where so little happens to relieve the monotony, news like that travels faster than the current. He didn't know what to make of it. Surely I have not seriously offered my life as guarantee for the delivery of a man I have never met?

Of course not, I said. How could I be so stupid?

With that out of the way we returned to more mundane matters. He is surprised how far the river has withdrawn since he was last here. O Varayo is looking, he said, like an abandoned wayside halt along a discontinued railway line.

It was irresistible to embellish the image. 'I am the station master,' I declared, 'for whom the trains no longer run.'

He smiled, thinking I meant the plantation.

Through the window we looked out on a dried-up channel

with a narrow stream threading down its length, barely enough for the dug-out canoes in which the Indians pole themselves to whatever miserable plots of fruit orchard have been left to them.

He reminded me, needlessly, what this would add to my transportation costs. I had already figured that out. The rubber will now have to be delivered by hired trucks to the next port of any significance, which is Paromante, nearly a hundred kilometres downstream.

The costs he quoted were sufficiently close to my calculations for me not to query them. Whatever percentage he is adding for himself can be barely enough to cover the effort of arranging it.

With business out of the way, he sat back expectantly, waiting to hear my gossip. I had none worth relaying and little heart for what he would trade in exchange. Nevertheless I sat patiently through his accounts of happenings in Guarameros, where the government is opening up an area the size of Portugal along the borders of the Mato Grosso to anyone who wants a part of it. Anyone, that is, except the indigenous Indians who – if FUNAI can get there in time to save them – will be herded into a fraction of what had been theirs since the earliest prehistoric migrants first hunted these forests.

I feigned interest and tried to smother the memories that image has always evoked, of another people gathered up and transferred *en masse* across country to clear the way for a 'superior species'.

No wonder those of us who managed to get away, before the Allies sealed off our escape routes, have always felt at home in this country. We were a people who understood the impulse to expand one's *Lebensraum*.

Alberto is not old enough to remember the war, not objective enough to see what is happening here. To him this is progress, development, the exciting vista of a new life, of a country surrendering its riches to those bold enough to take what can be theirs.

It pleases him to think that this is the last frontier. The only place left in the world where one can experience this kind of excitement. He thinks himself lucky to be of his generation, to be part of it before the last of the land is parcelled out and spoken for.

Useless to ask him about the Indians. What have they ever done for this country?

He looks upon me as an exemplar of the lifestyle he admires. A man who came here with next to nothing and turned the land to profit. He sees in me the essence of the pioneer spirit, one who knows far more than he reveals, who has tasted the rawness of the jungle before the first blade fell. Is it possible that I should tell him now why the axes must be put away and the jungle left in peace?

When the time comes to leave he smiles at me affectionately. 'See you next year.'

'Next year, yes. God willing.'

After he had gone I took my bottle and sat out on the elevated terrace, under whose cracked and gaping floorboards I had so often watched the river running at full spate.

I have never been at ease with the river. On others it has a calming effect, representing both the source of life and the conduit to the everlasting sea that awaits them at the end of their voyage. To me it is a source of danger and a reminder of my mortality. I feel its restless brown currents fretting at the edge of my shrunken world, ceaselessly eroding and bearing away this lingering remnant of who I am, threatening to undermine the façade I have endeavoured to display and expose the secrets buried beneath.

To be at peace with the river it is necessary to wade out and embrace it, allow it to wash over you, removing the dirt and revealing the underlying truth. Like those who are baptised into new faiths. Like aged Hindus who yoke themselves to pots and float downstream, waiting for the vessels to fill and submerge them in the sacred stream of eternity.

I seek death, yes, but I lack the courage to go out and meet it. To do that one must have faith in one's salvation.

And yet I have long sensed that the river, one day, will bring me my Nemesis.

Even though it has now retreated, leaving this dried-up watercourse where the jungle is already beginning to encroach. It may take a century to return, or it may be back with the next flood, blasting through the barriers of dead trees that diverted it into its present channel.

2

The population of O Varayo was never more than two thousand at most. Its only claim to existence lay in the fact that it was the last navigable port on this tributary, and the jumping-off point for those forging even deeper inland along the track which the foresters had carved, heading for the distant hills more than two hundred kilometres south of here.

The local shopkeepers made their living from supplying provisions to these settlers, advertising the fact that this was their last chance to equip themselves for their new life.

I used to sit on that very terrace, watching boatloads of would-be farmers and prospectors, from the slums of Manáus and Rio, decanting into the waiting pick-up trucks, lifting their children and hurling their bundles over the sides to claim their places away from the tailboards where rutted roads and clouds of dust would ensure the worst of the long ride. Watching the wives sent scurrying frantically to the nearest stores, with minutes in which to spend their meagre savings as wisely as they could.

In the worst of the rains, the road would be reduced to a slippery, glutinous facsimile of the river from which it deviated, providing a journey far worse than the immigrants had experienced so far.

Yet the influx continued in all weathers, and I never saw the same volumes in the returning traffic. How could the jungle continue to absorb such punishment? Where did they go? What lives did they find? What did their children remember of their origins?

At least they had lives to go to, I reminded myself. In that one crucial fact lay all the difference between them and the thousands I had marshalled through my yards to the waiting cattle trucks.

Scenes as fresh in my mind as if I saw them yesterday.

As if one embarkation began where the other left off, so that I must struggle to recall which led to hope and which to despair.

O Varayo is drying up, like the river bed, shrinking from neglect and from the decision, by the big forest combines, to follow the river and bypass us with the new road now under construction.

The river is a fickle, capricious thing, a painter never satisfied with his landscape, forever laying down new brush-strokes and obliterating old outlines.

The tradesmen lack the faith of Father Lorenzo. True, the river may return one day, but by then they will be dead. They are saving what they can and moving on themselves, still loyal to the river, following where it leads. For most it provides the only life they have ever known.

Now that they are going, leaving in this backwater only the handful who are too old and dispirited to make the change, I will come here more often. And I will bring Eduardo with me, to watch the twilights drag their last thin strands of reflection down the waning stream, the flights of macaws seeking their roosts in the far treeline. And perhaps a solitary Indian, leaning on the pole of his dug-out, silhouetted against contracting pools of magenta.

We will play at imagining that this is still the forest it was. His forest. His inheritance as it should have been.

He is fast expanding his vocabulary, but understands far more than he can speak.

The other day I was with him in the music room, explaining what it was I heard calling to me above the background noises of the jungle outside. I described it as the singing of the leaves. The leaves were singing my old songs to me from another land.

He understood immediately, picking up a dead leaf that had been swept by the wind within reach of us. Holding this to his ear, he smiled.

I shook my head. No, not like that. This leaf could no longer sing because it had fallen from the tree. If he wanted to hear the songs the tree had for him, the ancient songs of his tribe, he need only do what I did. Sit where we were and listen to the breeze gently skimming the leaves, plucking them like the strings of a harp.

He sat, and he listened, and slowly the smile came back to his face. And he nodded.

3

Father Lorenzo thinks that in protecting Eduardo I am defeating my objective. I am not preserving the glory of Rousseau's natural man but creating an unnatural hybrid less in tune with the reality of his times than the Indians who hang around the settlements feeding on the scraps of civilisation.

'You are deceiving yourself,' he said. 'You are bringing him up to believe in an ideal world that doesn't exist and never did. And what, after all, is so desirable in the world you open up to him? You want him to play Debussy and Ravel? To whom?'

'You miss the point,' I replied. 'I am teaching him what life can be before the time comes when he must learn what it is.'

'The disillusionment when he sees the difference will be more cruel than anything his simple kinfolk have experienced. They have looked up at us from the depths. He will have to descend from the heights.'

I shook my head. 'You still don't understand – do you? – that it is we and not they who inhabit the depths. By contaminating them, we drag them down with us.'

'Either way, our world is vastly different from that to which you will have him aspire. You are blinding him to the hard facts of life.'

'I will teach him, when the time comes, to make that transition. I will unveil the reality a step at a time.'

'You may not be here. To be frank, you have undertaken a task you will not be around to complete.'

I couldn't answer that. He is right, of course. I have allowed myself to be carried away without thinking through the consequences.

'Release him,' said the priest. 'Turn him free to find his own way. Let him grow up as an Indian child, which is, after all, what he is. It is only your love for him that makes you see some infant prodigy. If you really love him you will not be so selfish as to fashion him in your own likeness. Only God has that right.'

Their incontestable logic didn't make his words any less brutal. I hated him for being so wise, for voicing the misgivings that have been nagging in my own conscience.

Eduardo hasn't had a playmate of his own age, leave alone his own tribe, since he was born into this house. He has had only his parents and me.

What a strange environment I have created for him. A music room that transmutes light into sound! A piano that recalls the world of the French impressionists! A syllabus to teach him that thunder brings wonder and lightning is anything but frightening!

He is being raised by a child. A regressed adult who uses him to re-create his own lost childhood.

And who, as Lorenzo points out, will not be around to stay the course.

I must find the strength to ease myself from the hold he has on me, before he suffocates in my embrace.

DIVERTISSEMENT

I

I return to this journal after an absence of nearly two weeks, during which I have been absorbed in a discovery that has distracted me from all else.

We have stumbled, Eduardo and I, upon a cache of letters and papers concealed in the escritoire by the previous occupant of this house, and I have amused myself putting together, in the best traditions of Sherlock Holmes, a portrait of the man.

This fresh discovery came just two days after the murdered girl was found in the smallholdings, almost as if it were calculated to provide a much needed diversion upon which my mind could fasten.

It is Eduardo really who deserves the credit. Incessantly those tiny fingers probe and explore every nook and cranny of his world. It was inevitable he should spring the secret panel in the side of the desk, just below the roll-top compartments for stationery and writing instruments.

Why the owner should have seen fit to hide his trivial memorabilia, when there is naught there of anything but sentimental value, must remain a mystery. But that he set such store by it suggests some truth to the tales of his disappearance. The manner of which must have been so abrupt that it allowed no time to dispose of this meagre trove.

Principally it consists of letters from a woman signing herself Hélène, bearing postmarks ranging over the years 1937 to 1940 and stemming from an unspecified address in São Paulo. She could hardly have distanced herself further from O Varayo and still have remained in the country.

All these years her letters have been lying here, beside the chair in which I have spent so many hours in meditation, and I never knew.

Would it have mattered if I did? I doubt it. A twelve-day wonder, perhaps, which is all it has finally proved to be.

Mildew has caused the outer layers of bundled envelope to rot and decompose until they are no longer legible, but the rest has been reasonably well preserved. So much so that even now, after nearly fifty years, the earliest of them still impart a faint aroma of something other than decay, arousing a trace of guilty conscience as I gently pry their pages apart.

The tone of the letters is plaintive, querulous, expressing no interest in, or concern for, the health and welfare of the recipient. I see the latter cast in the role of abandoned husband, waiting anxiously for the long river journeys to deliver yet another rebuff or remonstration.

'You think it is enough', she writes, in English which I suspect does not come easily to her, 'to buy me a piano and sheets of music. So you want me to sit all day and play Debussy while you are out growing rubber? And for whom do I play this music? Do you want me to charm the wild creatures of the forest? Or those ugly savages who wear no clothes and smell like *merde*?

'You say you love me. If you love me you will leave that terrible place and take me back to civilisation. Do not suppose that piano music and views of distant forests will be enough to keep me in your jungle.'

Clearly he must have persevered with his entreaties, for her rebuttals become sharper and more pointed with each letter. She is not sure how much longer she can endure even São Paulo, whose climate is endangering her health. Besides, the news from Paris is extremely worrying. War might break out any moment and leave her stranded on this godforsaken continent. If he does not join her soon she will return to Europe alone.

Then comes a change. Suddenly she is asking why he has not written. She has not heard from him in three weeks. Is he ill? Is anything wrong? Why doesn't he answer? She needs more money.

He can't expect her to live on the wages he pays to his rubber tappers.

The letters become more anxious. She cannot understand why his last note, when it finally arrived, was so cryptic. Almost as if he were concealing something from her. She will not be treated like this, as if she were a mistress from whom he withholds more than he is willing to reveal.

At this point my interest quickens. I warm towards my predecessor, alone in this house with his specially imported Bechstein, tortuously conveyed here at God knows what cost and peril to its marvellously exotic construction. I read on in hopes that he has at last provoked in her some appreciation of what she is in danger of losing.

But no. The panic is there, yes. And rising. Yet still she is the wronged woman, paying the price of his insensitivity to her needs and his determination only to please himself. At one stage she has considered booking passage upriver to catch him in his infidelities. For she is by now convinced that he has taken to bed 'some dirty native bitch'.

Then she changes her mind. Her money is running out. By chance, someone has come to her rescue. Someone who has shown her greater understanding and affection in a fortnight than she has received from him in four years. Her saviour is a fellow countryman who, like her, was unfortunate enough to be cast upon this hostile coast. Of all the men she has met here, he is the only real gentleman. Soon he will return to fight for the Free French, and she will be sailing with him.

Au revoir, Bernard.

Of all the men she has met here . . .

How many?

And under what circumstances?

I seize, as Holmes would do, upon this revealing detail.

Did Bernard already know? Had he guessed? And was that why the flow of correspondence dried up?

Bernard Reynald. Was he French, I wonder, or English? Or a bit of both?

English, I fancy. Why else should her letters struggle with that language? Why else the library of Conan Doyle? And the naïve assumption that if he bought her a piano, and a stack of pieces by French composers, she would be content to share his wilderness?

I am saddened by this prosaic explanation for the existence of the Bechstein. I had pictured something much more grandly romantic.

What became of him? Was she right about the native mistress? And if so, on receiving the news that she was contemplating the river journey to catch them out, did they run away together into the forest?

Surely not, for the next letter signalled her removal from their lives. Yet this too was consigned to the secret panel of the escritoire.

Perhaps Bernard, jealous of his rival, and shamed by his commitment to a patriotic cause, succumbed to similar sentiments and, leaving the house and plantation as they stood, without so much as a word to his peons, took ship himself to the distant war in Europe. So readily abandoned, the Indian mistress would have to choose between returning in disgrace to her tribe or, unable to bear that humiliation, drowning herself in the river.

Another history swallowed without trace by the all-obliterating jungle, where evolution has so refined the art of scavenging that a corpse can be consumed entirely within days, leaving only the bones to sink into the humus.

2

Father Lorenzo came to see me. He heard about my promise to the tribe. He begs me either to inform the authorities of the case, so that they can mount a proper manhunt for the killer, or to send him as my representative to negotiate new terms. He realises the tribe must be appeased somehow, but it is madness, he says, to offer myself as scapegoat for a crime committed without my knowledge, by a stranger I have never set eyes upon.

I wish he hadn't come.

He has started up afresh within me a gnawing unease like a

nagging toothache. A year is a long time, yet he has managed to make it seem more like a week.

Father Lorenzo has nicotine stains in his beard and fingernails. I tell him he is as much in danger of dying from lung cancer as I am from an arrow tipped with the sap of the *tiki uba* tree. But he does not appreciate my levity, which he describes as ill becoming a man recklessly gambling with his life.

Suicide, he warns me, is a sin.

How I wish I could explain to him how lightly that sin would sit upon me after all that has gone before.

Why, he asks, have I placed myself in this situation?

I point out that I am old. Old enough to have fathered Father Lorenzo. And my world is steadily narrowing to an even finer focus than that to which it has been restricted for the past forty years.

But again this only arouses his curiosity, and he returns to the line of enquiry he has fruitlessly pursued through many such conversations.

So that once more I throw the question back at him. Why is *he* here?

His sad eyes, under their shaggy brows, look accusingly back at me. How can I have failed to understand, after all the time we have known each other, that he is merely fulfilling his duty to help the Indians?

I shake my head. 'Come on, admit it. We are simply here, both of us, because we are world weary. We envy the Indians. They have preserved the essential humanity that we lost long ago.'

He professes bewilderment. How can I even suggest such a thing? These are primitive, godless people.

'Whom you want to protect from the highly advanced killers we have become,' I point out. 'To the extent that you have even suggested the only way to save them is for all of us to pack up and leave.'

Yes, he admits he said it, but I have misunderstood him. He meant only that our complex civilisation is too much for the Indians ever to grasp. And in failing to come to terms with it they will die.

'You try to convince yourself that you are protecting them

from their inability to change. Because you dare not confront the truth. The condition to which our own ability to change has reduced our so-called civilisation. We have *not* gone forward but backward. Not hand in hand with God and the angels but step by step with Satan and his hordes. It is *we* who have become the savages of this planet.'

He can see there is no point in arguing with me. Stimulating as it may be to engage in theological debate, he is not equipped to lock horns with the Devil himself. He knows the jibe cannot hurt me. For this is all familiar terrain, in which we return to our opposing positions with the enthusiasm of schoolboys lobbing toy grenades.

'The trouble with us, Father Lorenzo, is that we both want the same thing. Only your religious beliefs will not allow you to admit it. You speak of my risking the mortal sin of suicide. And yet you seek no less. You crave redemption for the ancient sins of Portugal and for the bloody path your people have carved through this continent. And you seek it through your personal, private crucifixion. But who is to drive in the nails? The natives? It is not their sins you bear. The trespassers, then? For surely they are the real transgressors here?'

The good Father is appalled. Am I aware of the sacrilege that slips so easily from my tongue? 'Tell me,' he counters. 'Whose sins do *you* bear?'

I smile. 'My own, Father. Only my own.'

If I am not afraid for myself, what about my obligation to the child I profess to love?

He has me there. I should never have admitted it to him. In a moment of silly, mawkish weakness, during a visit months ago when he found me engaged in some foolish game with Eduardo, I exposed my Achilles' heel.

Love!

What a fatally incriminating word! To be wrung from the lips only under extreme duress. And even then never in such a way as to identify the object of that emotion.

Only once before did I lay myself open to the hidden but ever-present Furies that followed me here. When I decided I would marry Imelda.

Her gravestone was lichened before Father Lorenzo ever set

foot in O Varayo. How can he know that she paid for my sins? That, like Judas, I betrayed her through the simple act of publicly embracing her, thus allowing the Furies to fall upon her like vultures?

She died with the child stillborn in her, and there was no doctor to say why, no priest to comfort me, no logical explanation to dispel the terrible conviction that she was taken from me simply because I had tempted providence.

I swore then that if I ever loved again I would guard that secret even from the loved one. Deny it even to myself.

But the years have lowered my guard and lulled my apprehensions. Once again I am endangering a life by allowing myself to love. And allowing others to know it. Even recording the fact in the pages of this journal which I conceal, superstitiously, in the escritoire.

Look at poor Bernard Reynald. He thought the letters would be safe here. Yet I am reconstructing a portrait of him which his own demons – were he still alive – might pounce upon and deliver to the flames.

3

Today is Good Friday. To please Father Lorenzo, I attended the Stations of the Cross. I never attend Mass. Why should I endure to watch others granted the absolution that cannot be mine?

The chapel is a clapboard affair set on a slight rise above the waterfront shacks. Father Lorenzo delights in the fact that the building was constructed and furnished by the voluntary efforts of his parishioners. And is especially proud of the Stations, carved by a local carpenter who had never before attempted such bas-reliefs.

His work betrays this, but also possesses a certain beauty in its naïvety. The face of Christ dominates each panel; two lines angled upward to suggest eyes closed in suffering, and a mouth half open in a rictus of pain. Other figures crowd around the edges of the scenes like vicious Lilliputians baiting a Gulliver. Somehow the ordeal inflicted by these tiny, individually insignificant figures is all the more harrowing.

Estancia, I know, does not like these replacements for the cheap, faded but homely prints she knew as a girl. She especially misses the sad face of Christ gazing at his mother. The face that looked compassionately upon her own perilous arrival into the world. She claims she might not have survived under the squeezed up, slanting eyes of this wooden Christ.

I try to follow with my rosary, step by step, bead by bead, Father Lorenzo and his flock down the road to Golgotha. I struggle to communicate my private entreaty, not for myself but for Eduardo. Having revealed his name, I pray the child will be spared the punishment due, not to him, but to me.

Take me, Christ. Take me.

But even here the Devil whispers in my ear. Study that face. What is his suffering compared with the suffering you have seen? How dare he imagine that his death was so great as to compensate for all the others that have died. Remember what you yourself have witnessed. The faces crowding the doorways of the freight cars, resigned to an end far more protracted, far less merciful than his one afternoon on the cross. Recollect what you yourself achieved, in response to a single phone call. The order that led to the extinction of more than a hundred in just a few minutes of blind panic.

Remember that. Make yourself remember that. And then ask yourself, what is this compared with that? Recall the detail. The woman who stumbled with her child, holding him out towards you as she went under, screaming, 'Save him, save him.'

And you ask this Christ to take you, and spare the child? At least the child she offered up was her own. What is Eduardo to you that you should presume the possibility of his salvation?

When the service was over I stayed behind to compose myself while the congregation filed out into the sunlight. But Father Lorenzo had spotted me. He came over and said, 'I am happy to find you here. I was watching you. I could see that you were moved. It is never too late for the sinner to rediscover the love of Christ.'

Oh yes, Father, I thought. Oh yes it is.

FUGATO

I

An inquiry was held to determine the cause of the 'incident'. For among the dead were two of the guards, crushed underfoot in the mêlée.

I waited in the reception room of the town hall, where the proceedings were conducted. I would be the next one called to give evidence.

Also waiting was the girlfriend of one of the deceased guards. I had seen her around the station once or twice, arriving on her bicycle to seek him out, always bringing with her some special treat she had cooked for him. They were engaged to be married.

She had volunteered her services as a witness, although why her offer was accepted I could not imagine. She wasn't even there when the stampede took place.

She looked at me strangely without troubling to conceal her hostility. The rumour was abroad in the town that I was the one who gave the order. That I had somehow got it into my head the Führer was passing through on a tour of inspection.

Where could such a report have originated?

Through the window I could see the boarded shopfront of a bakery across the street, still bearing the faded chalk outline of the Star of David with the words *'Juden Raus'*.

It was said there were no Jews left in this part of Bavaria. That we had managed to get rid of them all.

My turn came. I was ushered into the council chamber, warmed by a pot-bellied lead stove in the corner.

The panel consisted of four: two military and two civilian. I did not recognise any of them, and knew nothing of their credentials.

I was asked to be seated and reminded that these proceedings were not in the nature of a trial, but merely an investigation into the circumstances of the 'incident'.

I was asked to describe in my own words what had led to the order to clear the tracks.

I told them. That even though I did not ask for the identity of the caller, the urgency in his voice was enough to convince me I had only minutes to spare before the arrival of the train.

Was it conceivable that the Führer's train might actually be travelling this line? The tone of the questioner was not sarcastic. He merely wished to know the likelihood of such an eventuality.

I said it was unlikely, but the vehemence of the order I received had led me to accept it was conceivable, yes.

Did the caller say where the train was proceeding?

No. Nor would it have been possible for me to ask. One did not challenge such orders.

Was there any reason why an anonymous caller would wish to convey false information of this kind?

I could think of three.

He was jealous of my appointment, and of the responsibility I exercised at such an early stage in my career.

He was a Jew hater who, knowing the tracks would be filled with evacuees in transit, hoped to produce precisely the chaos that had arisen.

He was a security officer testing the system to see how its personnel reacted under stress.

The panel were interested in the last of these possibilities. If that were the case, how would I rate my performance?

I replied that I had clearly failed the test.

I requested that I be relieved of my responsibilities and dismissed from the service.

Quite out of the question, they replied. I must be aware of the drain on manpower and the urgent need for experienced officers like myself to operate the system.

In that case, let me at least be posted somewhere else, to another station.

But that too would not be possible. It would take time to find and train a replacement, and mine was a key post in this sector.

What, then, was their verdict? I asked.

It was not for them to pass judgement but merely to sift the evidence and submit their report. They had other witnesses to question and it would take time to complete their deliberations.

Meanwhile I was to return to my post and continue with my duties. Being careful, in future, to check the identity of anyone who might phone through with urgent instructions to impart.

I was about to leave when one of the civilians, a stout man with glasses, asked why it had taken so long to remove the bodies from the tracks and restore normal services.

When I said we were short of stretchers he wondered why we hadn't simply piled them into the freight cars and shunted them out of the way.

2

I toy with the letters left in the escritoire.

I compose imaginary missives to insert between those that came from Hélène. On Bernard's behalf, I appeal, I entreat, I cajole.

My dear, sweet Hélène, you cannot begin to conceive the torture I endure without you. Every time I see the keyboard, I hear your delicate fingers rippling the notes, brightening the evening with the colours of Debussy.

Oh, you are wrong, so wrong, to accuse me of harbouring a mistress. There can be no one but you in my heart. There never has been, ever since I met you. And to suppose that a mere native would substitute for your inimitable charms is to do me the gravest injustice.

How can I convince you of the beauty of this place?

From the front door, you can see across the cultivated gardens of rubber, stretching in lines as straight and regimented as the gardens of Versailles, to a prospect no less distant and grand.

It is a view to remind you, my dear, of the vineyards of Provence, laden with the sound of bees and the rich autumnal scents of the harvest.

Oh, come to me, Hélène, I beg you. Your latest letter leaves me writhing with desire. I clutch and rend the sheets. I am eating the pillows! The feathers fill my mouth, and still I think only of you. Of your plump thighs, your voluptuous breasts, the matted wedge of your pubes rich with the texture of honey.

Do not forsake me, my poppet. Your Pattacake is pricking with lust for you.

And then, later:

You bitch! You strumpet! You French whore! Your latest letter has sent me on a rampage of destruction. I have destroyed every photograph, every reminder of your evil, scheming face.

You dare to accuse me! And all this time you have parted your legs for the scum of São Paulo.

I took an axe to the Bechstein, within an ace of bringing it down upon the spotless keys. Ivories that came so close to being stained by your podgy, deceitful paws. What tunes have those fingers stroked? Not Ravel or Debussy, I fancy, but the groans of beasts in their rutting.

I spit upon you, Gallic strumpet!

And yes, you were right. I have a mistress. A creature of the forests infinitely more gracious and beautiful than any your kind has ever produced. I no longer chew the pillows. I nibble her ear and make her laugh with my descriptions of your elephantine cavortings that masqueraded under the name of sex.

And I play her Ravel and Debussy and teach her that it is possible to salvage, from the chaos of the selfish world you still inhabit, some fragment of the spiritual fulfilment for which civilised man has striven with such little success.

I especially delight in amusing her with the 'Golliwogg's Cakewalk', and the picture it conjures of you strutting the streets of São Paulo.

3

The escritoire holds other secrets, in a compartment which even Eduardo has not found.

Principally a store of clippings from newspaper reports and magazine articles treating the trial and execution, by hanging, of Karl Adolf Eichmann.

This evening, with the child in bed and the generator already illuminating the main wing of the house, it is time, once again, to remember. So I stay behind in the candle-lit music room to sift through the yellowing layers of newsprint. And I marvel, afresh, that I am still waiting, after twenty-seven years, for the inevitable sequel.

What was Eichmann, after all, that I was not? He did no more than organise the transportation. I did no more than contribute my share towards the execution of those arrangements. I helped to keep the traffic flowing.

I will say it now, admit it now, in the pages of this journal. For what terrors are left, after all this time, that I have not lived through again and again, in a myriad vigils such as the one I hold tonight?

Even if I were the last one left alive, I cannot forget. Cannot allow myself to forget.

So I pick through the tattered clippings one by one, beginning with his arrest on 11 May 1960, near Buenos Aires, by Jewish 'volunteers', who smuggle him out of Argentina, nine days later, to Israel. Next comes the protracted controversy over this violation of Argentine law. What right have the Israelis to try this man whom they have forcibly abducted from his place of domicile?

But try him they do. Before a special court in Jerusalem at which three judges preside. And where history's bones are exhumed for display to the cameras of a world that has discovered the international intimacy, immediacy and instancy of television.

Throughout the harrowing testimony of the survivors, who outlived or outwitted the gas chambers, firing squads and charnel houses of Auschwitz, Belsen, Buchenwald and Dachau – to select from just the first four letters of the alphabet – the cameras remain fixed on the seldom varying features of the man in his box of bullet-proof glass who was 'merely carrying out orders'.

Yet it is soon evident that this isn't the trial of one man. This is mass catharsis through enforced recall. The human race grabbed by the scruff of its collective neck and pushed face down into the blood and the mire and the stinking, putrefying flesh of the six million who died so that Germany could 'cleanse its genes'.

This is the Jewish solution come full cycle; the show trial that makes the world remember that humanity did this. Has done it before, countless times, in a myriad contexts throughout history. And can do it again.

The trial drags on from 11 April to 15 December 1961, and Eichmann is sentenced to be hanged. His appeal is heard in March 1962 and judgement given at the end of May. His defence counsel, Robert Servatius, contends that only when the accused is able to examine the entire record of the case against him, at his leisure, can he 'remind himself of what his exact doings have been'.

Servatius also contends that the psychological approach of Eichmann's judges must have been affected by the tragedy of the 'final solution', especially as they themselves lost relatives during that operation. The situation should be viewed in the context of the wartime dictatorship in which the accused operated. 'The guilt,' he says, 'lies with the rulers and the system of rule!

'The accused,' he adds, 'does not present any danger whatsoever. On the contrary, he might constitute an instrument for the obviation of dangers.'

The court of appeal confirms the sentence imposed by the district court. It sustains the view of Eichmann's personal responsibility and, while conceding that no sentence passed upon him can be proportionate to the enormity of his crimes, says this 'dare not move us to mitigate the punishment'.

The court concludes its judgement by referring to the historical significance of the entire trial. 'The fact that the appellant by a variety of ruses – escape, hiding, false papers etc. – succeeded in evading the death sentence that awaited him, along with his comrades, at Nürnberg, cannot afford him relief here, when he at last stands his trial before an Israeli court of justice.'

His appeal rejected, Eichmann applies to the president of Israel for mercy. This application is rejected and, within three days of the appeal's dismissal, Eichmann is hanged.

The execution is carried out on 31 May 1962, and Eichmann's ashes are scattered in the sea, 'to prevent his grave becoming a place of pilgrimage'.

How will I, when my own time comes, face my executioners?

In fear and trembling? With cries for mercy on my lips? Or with the peace that comes from knowing I have no further distance to run and no more need to hide?

4

One of Eduardo's teeth was misaligned. While Estancia held him, Esquamillo knocked it out with a stick to prevent it deforming his mouth. It would have fallen out eventually of its own accord, because it was one of his milk teeth. But meanwhile it could have disturbed the roots of the others.

The *seringueiros* gathered round, laughing. But not with any malice, for they were showing the boy how to make light of it.

Eduardo cried out only once, and then proudly held up the offending tooth, his mouth still streaming with blood.

It hurt me just to watch, but I forced myself to do so.

He is their son and they must bring him up according to their custom.

Besides, the nearest dentist is in Paromante. And to sit in his chair, trapped in metallic arms and surrounded by surgical implements, would have been for him by far the greater ordeal.

At times like this I worry that my anxiety shows on my face. That he will detect it and wonder why.

He is a creature of this environment. I must accept that. He needs its dirt in his bowels and its germs to trigger his immunity.

I can give him music and an understanding of a wider world beyond this horizon. But I cannot inflict on him the kindly cruelties which will be necessary to temper his Indian sinews.

PURGATORIO

I

When I picture my own trial I am struck by the fact that I am surrounded by Jews, in a country which they control, where they issue and execute the orders.

And what people these are! What certainty, what self-assurance, blazes in their eyes! There is nothing they cannot do. The world is now theirs, and they are eating into it, little by little extending their boundaries and expanding their empire, while the rest of us watch, still consumed with guilt for what was inflicted upon their forebears.

Much has happened since they brought Eichmann to this court. A whole generation has grown up since then, spilling over their borders, pulling down the homes of those who dare oppose them. Not do as you would be done by, but as you *were*.

But no. My defence counsel tries to draw a parallel that has no validity. Nothing they do now can compare with what was done to the six million who died in the concentration camps.

Which is the point the prosecution seeks to establish straight away. The fact that these systematic eliminations were in progress long before Germany was at war, and that those of us in any way involved must have been fully aware of what was happening in the camps.

'You answer to the name of Kurt Hellmann?'

'I answer to the name of Kristian Hardy.'

'We realise that only the initials remain, but you once answered, did you not, to the name of Kurt Hellmann?'

'Yes,' I reply. Why have it dragged out of me when there is so much evidence to come? And yet I must give an account of myself, must get them to see what I did in the context of its place and time.

'You pride yourself on the fact that you were the youngest station master in Germany?'

'I did.'

'Your station was Blumenwald, was it not?'

'It was.'

'Describe to us in your own words the traffic that passed through your station.'

'Farm produce, agricultural equipment, casks of beer, some textiles and light manufactured goods. What you would expect of a small market town in rural Bavaria.'

'I was not referring to goods traffic. I was referring to human traffic.'

'The passengers too. Aside from a few tourists heading for the Danube and the Alps, most were local commuters: farmers, housewives, textile workers . . . '

'The prisoners, Hellmann. The prisoners. The hundreds of Jews who arrived each day. So numerous, so visible, that they were disembarked at dawn, not on your platforms but in the goods sidings where they would be less conspicuous to those decent, law-abiding commuters who travelled your line. What about them?'

'I knew only that they were destined for the concentration camps.'

'And what happened in those camps?'

'I do not know.'

'You do not know? Even *now* you do not know?'

'I did not know then.'

'You did not know that they were being murdered, scientifically annihilated, by the most economically efficient means available?'

'I did not know this.'

'We will be hearing testimony to the effect that, on average, four hundred and seventy prisoners were passing through the goods yards of Blumenwald each day. And the traffic was one way only. What do you – correction, what *did* you suppose was happening to these people?'

'I supposed that they were political prisoners, held in custody until other arrangements could be made for them.'

'Other arrangements? You mean arrangements other than mass murder?'

'Yes. Other arrangements.'

His words are emotive but they do not seem to be reaching the spectators. Even in the press gallery the response is bored, indifferent. One or two reporters have left already. There is nothing new in this for them. What does it have to do with the world of today? It belongs in the history books.

Please stay. Listen to this. It *is* important. History is but the present translated by time. It can come back in another form, another guise. It is with us still. People are dying even today. The grass now covers the sidings at Blumenwald perhaps, but only because the horrors have shifted elsewhere.

The prosecuting attorney has not left. He pursues his line of questioning.

'Four hundred and seventy people a day. Three thousand two hundred and ninety a week. One hundred and seventy-one thousand, five hundred and fifty a year. Where were they all going? Where could such numbers be accommodated until "other arrangements" could be made for them? Did you stop to consider the simple arithmetic of the equation, Herr Hellmann?'

'No, I did not. It was not my business to do so. I was a mere station master. My job was to see that the passengers were cleared and that the trains left on time.'

'Was that your job too where the prisoner known as Rachel Teller was concerned?'

Rachel!

Have they found her? Is she alive?

'Call Rachel Teller.'

She enters the court room, and even the yawning spectators crane their necks to see.

For she has not changed. Even in the forty-six years since I last saw her she has not changed. She is still *exactly* as she was then. More child than woman, with limbs as slender as an exquisite Dresden figurine.

Her eyes seek mine. Open, trusting, filled with bewilderment more than fear. Mine is the only face she recognises in this room, and hers the only one I have yearned to see again.

What a face! No supreme self-confidence there. No mastery of her fate and her world. None of the characteristics of those who claim kinship with her, who have brought her to this court room to symbolise the repression they have contrived to punish.

She is the very epitome of those who suffered. They could not have chosen better.

Or chosen worse. For Rachel has no place here. She does not belong among them. They are as much strangers to her as we were. She is out of step with their time, and they – God knows – are far removed from hers.

Hers is a vanished species. She is as they were, but can never be again. To see that face preserved in this age is to look upon the innocence of a lost youth which the world – the *collective* world, not just the German Reich – has set out to destroy and has very nearly erased from existence.

Hers was a species others seized on as ready-made for persecution. Because of the naïvety of their assumption that human horizons were boundless, that mankind was magnanimous. Which led them to wander with the candle of their culture bravely cupped against the chill darkness of unfamiliar terrain.

When the beasts sprang from that darkness, defending territorial boundaries they didn't realise they had crossed, they huddled together for the safety of whatever numbers they could assemble. Only to make themselves more conspicuous, more exposed. The ghettoes were built with their own hands. Once erected, they were so easy to daub with the vitriolic graffiti of their unforgiving neighbours.

We ask ourselves, what is it with the Jews? When we should be asking, what is it with us?

Why do they arouse in us the basest of instincts? Suspicion, mistrust, resentment, jealousy, and finally rage and blind, unreasoning violence?

They were put among us by God to test our patience and try our love for our fellow man.

And we failed the test!

No wonder that, now, their successors must punish us for that grievous flaw in our humanity. And show us what can happen when the boot is on the other foot! For the greatest sin of all is that we have robbed them of their innocence.

And if we can do it to them, we can do it to others. *Are* doing it to others. It isn't the survival of the fittest. It has nothing to do with that. It is the ugliness of the overdog. The impulse to snarl when we can afford to smile, to strike when we have no reason to do other than stroke, to sack when we should succour.

The irrepressible urge to victimise the vulnerable.

'Rachel Teller, do you recognise this man?'

She looks at me and nods her affirmation.

'Tell us, in your own words, how you came to meet him and what part he played in your life.'

But she is silent.

The court is suddenly wide awake, waiting for her to speak.

Tell them, Rachel. Tell them.

It can't hurt me now. And it might save you.

If only you could lance the wound and let the poison drain.

2

Esquamillo arrives with news for me. The killer of the Indian girl has been seen in O Varayo, boasting of the impunity with which he can come and go, laughing at the report that I am pledged to deliver him to justice.

He urges me to accompany him there and confront the man.

To what purpose? I ask. Is it likely that the man will meekly submit to punishment? Will he willingly accompany me to the tribal reserve and accept his execution?

Of course not, he replies. It will take force to accomplish this. But I am not alone. Esquamillo will be by my side, together with an escort of tappers from my estate. They will not see me harmed. The man will not stand a chance against our combined strength.

If I face him, I say, I will face him alone.

That is not possible, for this is not a cowboy movie. The man is a killer. He has the mind, and the reflexes, of a snake.

Very well. I will allow them to accompany me. But they must remain in the background while I make the overtures. They can come to my defence only if the man turns violent.

So we set off, five of us in all, with me dressed as formally as the occasion demands although, at my insistence, I remain unarmed while they carry the weapons. I am sure that all in O Varayo know we are coming. Even the macaws, in the trees lining the canal, rise and take flight at our approach.

He is no longer there, of course. He is gone. A display, as I suspected – and half hoped – of sheer bravado.

But to what purpose?

Why?

He has left me with my heart pounding and my years reeling through the picture frame of memory.

That it should all end here, like this, in the muddy, dirt-strewn main street of O Varayo, like some comic showdown from a dated Western. Denied my last words in the court of world opinion, my urgent reminder that, while we may be barely alive, and incapable of further crimes, the evil that we did lives on among us.

And will not be expunged with my death.

NACHTMUSIK

I

I have been ill. Some non-specific tropical virus which turned into pneumonia and left me so debilitated I wanted nothing but sleep. Esquamillo was worried enough to put a call out on the radio from O Varayo to the nearest doctor, based sixty kilometres away, on the first staging post of the southern highway.

When a description of the symptoms proved inadequate for a diagnosis over the air, the doctor promised he would look by on his next visit to collect supplies upriver.

That was six weeks ago, since when I have been slowly on the mend, and am now well enough to return to the music room and the escritoire.

Eduardo is once again following me around, but he senses a change in me. Painful as it is to do so, I keep this new-found distance between us. Perhaps the very first of a lifetime of disillusionments for him, but he has to start somewhere.

Lorenzo is right. He has become too dependent on me, and I on him.

Nearly three months have passed since I last wrote in this journal! And most of that time I have spent slipping from dream to dream, as a swimmer might from pool to pool. Would it were true that death is one endless dream from which we never awaken. If it is I will ignore the last trump and turn over in my sleep, hoping I will not be missed at roll call.

My slumbers bring no nightmares to compare with what I have witnessed in my waking hours. Sometimes they disassemble the elements of past horrors and present them in new forms, easing the trauma by reinforcing the unreality. At times I am filled almost with joy to discover in my dreams that things were not what I thought them to be. That the thousands who shuffled past in the dim light of the marshalling yards were bound not for the gas chambers and the lime pits but for some mysterious destination illumined with a radiance impossible to describe.

I almost envy them, wishing I could steal away from the limbo of the goods sidings and join their never-ending stream as they file onward into the swelling dawn.

Sleep is my surgeon, easing a delicate scalpel into my mind, cauterising the pain, suturing and reconnecting the wounded tissue, stitching together the threads of memory to present alternative views of the past.

A recurring theme is that Rachel never left me, that she was never removed from my quarters by the smirking guards and bundled off barefoot across the cinders to join the latest arrivals filing into the carriages. That instead she followed me here to sit with me in the music room. Sometimes I turn to her and catch the light from the leaves reflected in her smiling face, from which all trace of terror has been erased. And I can't believe how lucky we are to have escaped unscathed into this secret world where no one will ever find us.

Sleep is my cruel deceiver, surrendering me to the painful betrayal of my waking days where the nightmare *is* the inescapable reality. Where instantly that reality springs back into my mind, complete in every undeniable detail.

I remember again the shock of discovering her in my office closet when I went to don my greatcoat for morning inspection. Her eyes dilated with fear, and yet her lips curled more in a snarl than a scream, and her small fists clenched as if to strike back in self-defence.

Somehow, when her group was disembarked at dawn, she had crouched between the trucks, evading detection as she worked her way, carriage by carriage, towards the platform, heading for the station entrance. Thwarted by the presence of the guards at the gates, she had slipped into my office and taken refuge in the closet.

In the fraction of a second it took for me to figure out how she got there I heard the office door opening behind me, forcing me to a decision that changed my life, even though it only delayed the inevitability of hers. I could have called for the guards and had her removed. Instead I pulled out the greatcoat and closed the closet, turning to confirm that I was ready to join my military counterpart, the movements officer, for the embarkation procedures.

When I returned more than an hour later she was still there. And by now there was no turning back. After all I had inured myself to, it was not in me to add this one detail to the long list of tasks I had performed in the line of duty. Having raised her hopes, I couldn't be so callous as to hand her over to the fate she had tried so hard to evade. Besides, the train had already left. She had dropped out of the system.

I smuggled her through the connecting door to my quarters, cautioning her, quite unnecessarily in view of the skills she had so far displayed, to remain hidden under my bed, where I passed her my lunchtime sandwiches and coffee. She was like a rabbit, frozen in its bolthole with ears tuned to the sounds of predators, conditioned to smother so much as a whimper until the final capture released the vocal chords in one despairing shriek.

2

The traffic on the line was so heavy in those days that I had taken to spending all my time in the station, using the evenings to keep up with my records. There was nothing unusual about the fact that, when I wasn't on the platform, in the repair shed or somewhere in the sidings, I would be in my quarters, catching some rest. My staff knew better than to disturb me without knocking and giving me time to dress.

I thought about how to proceed from there, how to arrange for her to run the gauntlet of the guards to the world outside. But I thought too of what would happen if she got that far. And the more I thought, the more hopeless it seemed.

She was Hungarian! God knows how she had arrived, alone,

in this corner of the world, but there she was. Unable to speak a word of German. She was sixteen years old, half starved and trembling with fright. She wouldn't survive an hour in a Bavarian market town where a stranger from the next village was an object of curiosity.

There was no underground in Bavaria, no cell of resistance I could contact to organise an escape route. The room in which she had found refuge was her survival pod on the surface of an alien planet. I think she knew this from the start, could read the futility of her flight in my eyes.

Unable to communicate, except for the few odd words familiar to her, we resorted to gesture and mime, in keeping with the silence so necessary to our safety. She recognised what I was risking, sought to convey her gratitude for my unexpected act of humanity.

But was it humanity?

Or was I deceiving both her and myself?

Knowing all the time how pointless was this brief respite, why did I prolong the suspense? Wouldn't it have been kinder to spare her the agony of waiting and simply return her to the guards without further delay?

I only know that lying there beside her, staring into those trusting eyes, letting my fingers stray gently down those limbs as delicately sculpted as a porcelain figurine, I felt an exquisite pain in my breast and in my loins that overpowered my reason. And when I took her, and saw her eyes wince from the unexpectedness of it, I wouldn't have cared if the walls fell and the earth split to swallow us whole in that act of consummation.

Afterwards, when she sobbed silently in my arms, I stroked her hair, concerned that I had injured her. But she smiled through her tears and shook her head, indicating that she wept only for the proof of my compassion, for the discovery that this terrible world had at last yielded some capacity for love.

We tried to spin out the hours, disengaging from the tempo of our times as a carriage might be uncoupled to freewheel under its own velocity, coming to rest in a siding where the traffic would pass it by and the grass would grow over its wheels.

When we weren't making love we tried, with sparse vocabulary and much gesticulation, to converse. But mostly we had to fall back on music as our only common language. I would play for her, or else we would play together, seated side by side at the secondhand cottage piano I had installed beside the dresser. Stumbling upon a few works of Franz Liszt among my store of miscellaneous pieces, she was filled with childlike delight. Through sheet after sheet she barely depressed the keys for fear of bringing the guards to the curtained windows. She thought they would be able to distinguish between her playing and mine. And she was probably right, if they knew anything about music, for she was infinitely the better player.

Perhaps because of the tension of keeping so much in, her playing was marvellously controlled. Liszt *pianissimo*, performed as I had never heard him, delivered by one who was raised on him.

Even now, nearly half a century later, I cannot bear to play a note of his music.

All we were given was four days, which ended when, glimpsing her face briefly peering through the glass to watch for my return, one of the guards raised the alarm.

She looked back only once as they led her away. There was no accusation in her eyes. She had known this moment must come, and she would not give them the pleasure of releasing that final scream of anguish.

Nor could I cry out myself. I could only stand in the doorway, watching her, gripping the frame so hard my nails bit into the wood.

I wanted to be marched away myself, to be charged with aiding and abetting a prisoner to escape, to pay the penalty for betraying her. For being what I was.

But they laughed at me, as if my only crime had been to keep her to myself, like a greedy schoolboy who has stolen a box of chocolates. They nudged each other and whispered, the way all soldiers do when they discover the weaknesses of petty civilian officials who have avoided the draft.

Even the movements officer was barely polite when he expressed the hope that the interlude had provided a pleasant distraction from my routine.

When it was over, and the train pulled away under a pall of black smoke to deliver its cargo for extermination, I retreated into the room and locked the door behind me, desperate to find the means of inflicting the punishment I had been denied.

Taking a pair of scissors from the dresser, I tore open my shirt and stood in front of the mirror, slowly and precisely carving above my left nipple the mark of the swastika.

I wanted to be sure I would never forget who and what I was.

3

Few people have seen that scar, which time has slowly erased until it is now no more than a shapeless welt below the hairs of my chest.

Imelda saw it when it was still recognisable. It was a disfigurement difficult to reconcile with my fake Swiss passport and my claims to have worked as a courier for British intelligence.

I told her I had fallen under suspicion in the course of a mission across the border into Bavaria, and that my interrogators had branded me before releasing me, to discourage any disposition to such ill-explained sorties in future. I made light of it, amusing her by imitating their accents as they told me, 'Please remember, we have a war here.'

In those days we were all living in the aftermath of a war that had dominated our lives, no matter where in the world we happened to be. No one had escaped the knowledge of it, but it was seen by some as being also a period of excitement, containing even a measure of romance.

Rio was full of people who had stranger tales than mine to account for their exodus from the ruins of Europe.

I met her serving behind the counter of the bank where I called regularly to check on the arrival of transfers from my Swiss account. I had made the arrangements in the days of confusion that followed the Allied occupation, days that allowed a breathing space for those, like myself, who had good reason to emigrate.

From the frequency of my visits she acquired the misconception that I was wealthy, which I hastened to refute. When she finally consented to dine out with me I ensured that we did so in unpretentious surroundings. These excursions generally climaxed with tickets to the cinema, where my alleged English connections were reinforced by my ability to comprehend the American dialogue without recourse to subtitles.

She never invited me home. Her parents lived among the slum dwellers in the shanty towns proliferating even then in the hills above the city.

However, she did permit me to take her back to my hotel, where, gradually, I coaxed her into bed. She was not a virgin, and yet she would not have me think that she went to bed with anyone who asked her to dinner or to the cinema.

She told me she was twenty-one, but our marriage certificate recorded her as being barely eighteen.

Her parents came to the wedding, her father at least two shades darker than his wife and accompanied by three sons and four other daughters of every complexion in between. They were a close family, and even the father, a street sweeper, cried when we boarded the plane for Manáus. Perhaps they sensed they would never see her again.

We began our search upriver, in a series of voyages extending deeper and deeper towards that groin in the frontier with Bolivia and Peru. It was hard for her to understand why I was never satisfied with what we found. It was not that the properties were too expensive. Just that they were too accessible. But I couldn't explain to her the real reason.

We entered territory which, in those days, was considered far riskier than it is today, but if she felt afraid for our safety she never complained. She knew that some unaccountable force was driving me on; as mysterious as that cryptogram on my breast.

O Varayo was the furthest we could proceed by water, and we needed, if we were not to go completely wild, at the very least to be in touch with sources of supply to maintain our existence.

The abandoned house, reached along a narrow channel, with the stands of rubber already becoming engulfed in undergrowth on either side, stirred the same memory in both of us. The last film we had seen, in a flea-ridden cinema in Manáus, was *Gone With the Wind*, and we both remembered Scarlett's return to Tara.

When I addressed the group of smallholders we encountered on their way back from their morning rounds to collect the cups of latex, it was Esquamillo who stepped forward. A grinning boy barely in his teens, but proud to display the few words of English he had picked up – as I was to discover later – from Bernard Reynald.

My question as to who owned the house swept the smile from his face. He translated it for his companions, who looked at each other nervously and shrugged. None of them wanted to tell me, for it is bad luck to repeat the name of someone who has disappeared in mysterious circumstances.

They wouldn't even accompany us through the tangled vegetation that covered the driveway, but stood watching from a distance as I pushed open the door and saw, standing in the middle of the dark and musty hall, the Bechstein.

It was coated with a thick layer of dust, but its cover was propped up as if in readiness to release an enormous, resonating chord of welcome.

DIMINUENDO

I

I have come, slowly and painfully, to accept the fact that my marriage to Imelda was part of the continuing punishment I inflicted upon myself. And that the hurt was greater for her than it was for me.

Long before the Furies picked up my trail and pursued us here, she had begun to suspect this herself, and to draw apart from me. For fear that constant proximity would serve only to remind me of the cross I had chosen to carry with me into my self-imposed banishment from the world.

Perhaps this is too facile an explanation for the much more complex emotions that led us here.

I had, after all, loved her, if not for her looks at least for her inner beauty, her trusting nature and the delicacy of her limbs, reminding me so much of Rachel. Her mouth was wide and generous, her eyes always seeking opportunities to part it further in laughter.

I gave her too few such opportunities.

In our first months here we were much in each other's company. I would take her with me on my rounds of the estate, riding the horses we kept then in the half-ruined stables. I even permitted her to accompany me on explorations upriver, where she was ever on the watch for orchids and ferns she might bring back with us to decorate what she liked to think of as her rose garden.

She was an easy, restful companion, deferring to my initiative in embarking upon our conversations, quietly turning to her embroidery when I seated myself at the keyboard, ensuring that I was never troubled by the details of running that part of the mansion I had bothered to restore.

I cannot remember that she ever interrupted my thoughts to put a request or appraise me of a problem she might have encountered. She found other ways of ensuring that my attention was drawn to such matters and, if those failed, would resign herself to waiting until I could no longer ignore them.

If I considered then why I had chosen her as my companion, I would have said it was because she represented the antithesis of what we, in our Aryan arrogance, had sought to become. Hers was precisely the racial 'impurity' we had tried to purge from our midst.

It pleased me that she was dark and lissome rather than blonde and statuesque, Mélisande rather than Brünnhilde. She was at one with the depths of the forest, and the music of Debussy, rather than windswept heights and the posturings of Wagner.

Holding her in my arms, I would smile secretly at the futile vanity of our dreams of empire, in which white would have dominated every other shade. And the irony of the fact that the remnants of those who had indulged such fantasies were now driven to seek refuge in the most polychrome, polyglot nation on earth.

What sweet poetic justice.

But because I embraced the symbol, I remained blind to the real identity of the individual who had come to represent it. I failed even to perceive the fact that she, whom I looked upon as a creature of the wild, was in reality terrified of that wilderness, smothering the terror only for my sake.

It was Esquamillo who let slip, long after she died, the fact that, whenever I was away overnight, on business in Paromante or dealing with agents in O Varayo, she would send for Estancia, who was then just a child helping in the kitchen, to sleep with her.

I pictured them curled together in our bed, the slip of a woman from the city, frightened of every noise from the all-surrounding jungle, slowly lulled to sleep by the soothing gestures and crooning voice of an Indian girl barely half her age.

Steadily permitting myself to be engulfed by my increasing moods of despair, in those dark years of the late forties when German science and intellect were harnessed again to the perfection of new weapons for destruction, I ignored the effect upon her of these retreats into silence.

My self-castigation was almost unendurably painful to her. When I repaired to my lonely vigils in the music room, she would retire to the bedroom to kneel in front of the altar and pray for my dark soul while Estancia kept watch at the door.

There was at that time no priest available to replace Father Lorenzo's predecessor, who had died in his cassock – some said through too much fondness for sacramental wine. He it was who chose Estancia's whimsical name. Father Lorenzo, a much younger man, did not arrive until two years after Imelda's death.

Prayer was Imelda's only comfort. That and the perpetual flame I allowed her to keep alight on the bedroom altar.

2

The night she went into premature labour, there was no one but Estancia to help me. I knew nothing, and Estancia not enough. If I could have found the means to do so, I would have reached in to clear the blockage, cutting the child away to save her life, but we could only watch helplessly, applying hot compresses to her struggling, flailing body.

When the agony was too intense, and she slipped into a merciful coma, I offered a silent prayer of thanks, imagining the worst was over, not knowing that this was the only way it could end.

I have never understood why Estancia has not harboured hatred towards me, blaming me for Imelda's suffering. Instead she seems to have inherited Imelda's love, as though she had been given to understand that my own private purgatory surpassed all the pain Imelda would willingly bear on my behalf.

Not once did I ever reveal to my wife the origins of my affliction.

Not once did she ask.

She died knowing only that my demons, whatever they were, had caught up with me.

I buried her in the courtyard at the back of the house, where she had tried unsuccessfully to transplant the wild ferns and orchids we had brought back with us from the forest. And I sent a letter to her parents in Rio, from whom I received no response but a wreath of flowers. For years this withered garland adorned the tablet I ordered from Manáus, until the rains rotted it away.

By then the lichen had all but obscured the incised inscription, so eager were my Furies to deprive me of whatever scant consolation memory might keep alive of the few moments of genuine happiness we had shared.

AGITATO

I

Mental stimulus is my greatest need. My condition is that of a prisoner in solitary confinement. Other than Father Lorenzo, I have nobody from whom I can derive intellectual response. And with him there is always the stumbling block of religion. I feel him waiting like a patient policeman for my confession. Not to arrest but to free me.

He is my faithful dog, ready to follow me everywhere, if only I would let him. He watches my every gesture, biding his time until I drop my guard and accept him on my knee. He pants to lick away my sins.

It is not that I do not trust him. He could not betray me, even if I were Mengele himself. He is bursting with forgiveness, like a ripe plum, the juice of it running in his eyes.

But the burden of my guilt is too great for him to bear. I cannot have him, too, upon my conscience. It would destroy him. And he is too good a man to serve as just another scapegoat inflicted with the punishment meant for me.

So there are limits to what we can discuss, and when we talk my mind is busy closing doors rather than opening them.

This journal, then, has become my only refuge, my sole means of rationalising and structuring my thoughts, of making any sense of my long protracted existence.

I wish now that I had trusted myself to embark on it long ago. I could have eased the anguish if I had committed it to paper.

In these pages I have begun to rediscover myself, to come to terms with who and what I am.

And when the lock is broken on this cell in which I have confined myself, when the followers of Wiesenthal finally catch up with me, I will clutch this pathetic little record to my breast as they lead me to the stand.

It is the only evidence I have to offer. Even if it serves to incriminate rather than defend me.

What other witness can speak for me?

Father Lorenzo will doubtless be only too willing to say how much he loves me. Esquamillo and Estancia will perhaps testify to my credentials as an employer. But who else?

Who else is still alive?

And who will the prosecution find to speak for my wartime record? If I endure surely others have hung on long enough to point the accusing finger.

God, if only one of them were Rachel!

Just to know that she survived!

What is that saying the English have? Pointless crying over spilled blood?

Without Hitler, ours would have been an altogether different country. A Germany mercifully spared the delusions induced by his wild promises. We were drunk on the possibilities he spread before us. And, like drunken men, oblivious of the consequences of our acts. We hung upon his intoxicating rhetoric and did not hear the undertones. Our eyes were dazzled by the brilliance of the vision he dangled, and blind to the shadows it obscured.

And when at last we heard the nagging whispers, and saw the abyss opening up beneath the firmament, it was too late. We were already falling.

I have read somewhere that a minuscule change in our history, the failure perhaps of a single butterfly to keep its appointed destiny, would alter our surroundings beyond recognition. Everything is so finely tuned that the slightest shift of an element here, the displacement of an atom there, would profoundly affect the entire universe.

Germany without Hitler? Quite literally inconceivable.

I may not even have been born.

I am the product of my time, and will carry its stain as long as I live.

And yet, and yet . . .

Had the butterfly flown, had the atom shifted but a little, would I have fulfilled my destiny as I saw it in those heady years of my late youth?

I was a station master by profession. And proud of it. But my heart was set upon a career as a concert pianist. It was my hidden yearning, my secret dream. One for which circumstance had not prepared me and which my father's meagre means had denied me.

The secondhand upright which found pride of place in my tiny railside cabin was acquired as the means to that end. The hours devoted to its imperfect keyboard were an investment in my future. Until pressure of work compelled me to discontinue the practice, I took lessons three times a week from a Viennese music teacher named Altzheimer, whose faded newspaper reviews, framed over the Bösendorfer, lent some support to his claims as a one-time virtuoso.

Arthritis had forced him to transfer his technique from his fingers to his memory. And when he failed to instil it in me through attempts at thought transference, he stamped its rhythms with his feet and hammered them with his fist to accompany the ferocity of his commands.

Poor Altzheimer. Perhaps it was his method that defeated his purpose. By developing in me an aversion for the works of the composers he most admired, reduced to staccato toccatas and angry andantes. Not all of Brahms, Schumann and Schubert are as *Sturm und Drang* as he made them sound, but it took me a long time to discover that.

Would I ever have been a good, even a passable, pianist? How can I know? I have nothing against which to measure myself. I lack even a primitive phonograph on which to compare the recorded legacy of such masters as Backhaus and Schnabel.

Here I have only the night, the lanterns and the mosquitoes for an audience. Plus the occasional plantation worker or itinerant Indian who may pause in the darkness and wonder at the noise I make.

And of course Eduardo, the ever admiring Eduardo, who sits

with his feet dangling over the edge of the dining table, his lips slightly parted, watching me with rapt attention.

When I think of Eduardo, and of what he represents, I tremble with anxiety.

He is my last chance to leave behind something of value.

He has so many of my hopes riding on his tiny shoulders. I have made him too the bearer of a burden he cannot yet begin to grasp.

If the desert of my life could yield this one leaf!

I find when I write these things that my eyes mist over and I must pause to clear my vision. Why indulge in these futilities of imagination?

I would do better to emulate instead my fellow inhabitants of this rain forest, headed down the road to extinction and careless of the fact.

We are all hunted for different reasons. The tapir, the deer, the Indians who prey upon them and are preyed upon in return. Even the settlers who slash and burn and shoot to kill. They in fact are further down the road, among the ranks of the already dispossessed; the quarry of the bigger land grabbers who have driven them west.

This forest is dying, as are all who dwell in it. Even in the brief lifetime still left me I shall see it shrink further, to a vestige of what it was when I came, leaving soil too poor to farm and a heritage of failure and sorrow to those who destroyed it.

We are under sentence of death, and the sentence is almost written.

2

When I was a child, in Hamburg, my mother would take me to play in a park just outside the city, where stumps of wood were set upright in the ground to form patterns. I would leap from stump to stump, with the other children, trying to keep my balance. One day, as I grew a little older, it dawned on me that the stumps formed giant letters and numerals.

It came as nothing less than a revelation. I remember the configuration even now:

$$C_{12}H_{22}O_{11}$$

In all those years of treading upon it, I had not seen the grand design. And now that I did I could not comprehend its purpose. My mother could not explain it, nor could my father.

It was a mystery to us all, and I began to think of it as the fundamental equation of life itself, some eternal riddle posed by a deceased mystic, the equivalent of an Arthurian sword awaiting he who would wrest it from the ground.

It was not until my final year of study that I stumbled upon the solution in a chemistry text-book. $C_{12}H_{22}O_{11}$ was the chemical formula of sucrose.

Why it came to be there in that park on the outskirts of Hamburg I never did find out. A practical joker? Or just a landscape artist who had elected to honour, in this curious fashion, the Englishman John Dalton and his atomic theory of matter? Unwittingly leaving an impressionable youngster to adopt his cryptic creation as the key to life's supreme enigma.

When you learn that the key is a lump of sugar, there can be no more mysteries. And if we have to elect a metaphor for life itself, what better than that?

For the bitter after-taste of disappointment it leaves.

ERWARTUNG

I

My Nemesis has arrived.
I met her this morning when I went to O Varayo to purchase supplies from the one store still open for business.

She is staying at the Trocadero, the only guest they have had in months. I got to hear of her through the storekeeper. He was amused by the fact that Senhóra Remedios hurried to him to buy a fresh supply of sheets for the room they have opened and aired for her.

I called at the Trocadero to introduce myself, and my suspicions were aroused when she betrayed not the slightest curiosity as to what I am doing here. It is hard to define quite why I felt as if she had been expecting me.

Her name, she says, is Ruth Golding. She comes from New York and is allegedly here to study the butterflies of the upper Amazon basin.

Why, I asked, should they be any different here than they are in the rest of this wilderness?

A species, she explained, can vary considerably from region to region.

And how would she get to them, considering that most of them inhabit the upper layers of tree canopy and would never be seen from the ground?

She was prepared for that, having brought with her the equipment of a mountaineer to help her up the tree trunks. She took me to her room to show me. What Senhóra Remedios made of such brazen behaviour I can only imagine. It was a remarkable array of gear. Enough to scale the Andes if she ever got that far.

But it struck me also that it was the kind of apparatus a hangman would bring in order to set up a gallows in a public place. Ropes, clamps, pulleys, even a leather strap looking very like a noose.

Why else would she show it to me?

Was she intending to do this alone? I asked.

She planned to hire Indians to assist her.

I pointed out that locally, at least, the Indians are not great tree climbers. They haven't found it helps much in escaping their predators, who are pretty skilled at shooting them out of the branches.

She wasn't quite sure whether to take me seriously.

And what would she do if anyone started shooting at her?

Shoot back, she said, producing a Smith & Wesson Model 39 pistol. A weapon I had never seen before.

I am flattered.

I had not expected a Nemesis of such beauty. Straight from the legend. Daughter of Night and Goddess of Vengeance.

But if she *is* here to exact the retribution of angered deities, she betrays no sign of it in her eyes, which stare back at me with a disturbing candour and directness. As though she doesn't care if I know why she has come.

I have seen anacondas transfix their prey with the certainty of their death. Theirs are cold, cruel eyes that paralyse the victim with fright.

Not Ruth. Her eyes are cool but not cruel. They promise not pain but release.

2

I have not known such excitement in years. I am like a child who, after months of languishing on a sick bed, is promised a ride on a rollercoaster.

Even Eduardo is caught up in it.

Returning to the house, I gathered him up in my arms and said, 'Come on, we're going to look for butterflies.'

He knows what butterflies are. Esquamillo has taught him how to harness the giant morpho with the finest thread, trailing its vivid blue wings like a kite.

He has watched other species fluttering like wind-borne leaves into the music room, following the branches in search of nectar. They thrill him with their unexpected motions and colours. And he knows that, when we see them, we must hold our fingers to our lips and remain perfectly still, hoping they will alight on us.

Estancia is pleased that I am happy, that I am once again responding to Eduardo. She has not understood my motive in detaching myself from her son, who has been left to play alone at the rear of the house.

Who else is there for the boy to turn to? We are not exactly surrounded by armies of tribal urchins ready to take him out and scruff him in the mud so that he begins to understand the world on their terms.

Anyway, what harm can it do to spend with him what little time remains? He is young enough to recover from the parting. Children are resilient. Their bones mend fast and their scars are soon erased.

If he remembers me at all it will be through a familiar phrase of music in unlikely surroundings, evoking a mood, or a moment, shared with someone whose face he cannot quite bring to mind.

And yet, to some extent, I must prepare him, try to make it easier for him. I do not want to be guilty of yet another betrayal. He must know, somehow, that the time will come when we can no longer be together.

For the moment, however, we can think of nothing but butterflies.

But where to begin? I know nothing about them, and there is nothing in this house to help me. No word of them in the meagre library I have been left here. How I yearn for even the most abbreviated encyclopedic reference. How long do they live? How much ground do they cover in their life spans? How do they occupy their time?

Suddenly I am consumed with curiosity. Whatever her real

reason for being here, it would be unforgivable if Ruth were lying about her search for butterflies.

Perhaps I can find enough evidence of them here to attract her to the estate. It would make her task easier, anyway, if she is more concerned to find out about me.

3

This morning Eduardo and I extended our search, following the creek to its source way up beyond the back of the house. I haven't been that way in many years. The plantations that once existed there are long overgrown, reverting to secondary jungle.

At one point we paused and, through the trees, looked back on the house. Seen from the rear, the whole structure seems a ruin in which it would be impossible for anyone to reside. Shrubs are beginning to take root in the tiles above the stables, and there, unmistakably, is the tree which has invaded the music room, looking like a giraffe with its head stuck in a skylight.

I glance at Eduardo, anxious that his understanding of this will destroy our happy illusion of a secret sea beyond that inaccessible aperture. But he looks back at me strangely, as if concerned that it is I who must now suffer that loss.

I sense he has always known, and his eyes seem to be telling me not to worry. That the sea will always be there in our minds.

He can sometimes seem so much older and wiser than I. As if he draws upon some deep reservoir of tribal wisdom whose shores I could never hope to reach.

In the course of our quest we came upon a solitary giant of a mahogany tree standing unaccountably alone in a clearing and flooded with light, illuminated as though the victor of some primeval struggle for survival. About its spreading roots were scattered the decaying torsos of other trees that had succumbed to its superior strength. Spreading coronas of new foliage circled the conqueror's towering height, making it appear as though wreathed in crowns of laurel.

The scene was vaguely familiar to me, but I could not, at first, recall why.

Eduardo pointed to the tree and found a word he had stored in his limited vocabulary. 'Big,' he said.

I nodded. 'Big. But also old.'

He frowned slightly, as though wondering how a tree could be two things at once.

'Old,' I said, pointing to my chest and then back at the tree. 'Old.'

'Old,' he said, repeating the gesture, coupling me with the tree.

Indicating the rotting tree trunks that lay like sleeping green corpses on all sides, I gave him another word. 'Dead,' I said.

'Dead,' he repeated.

Only once before has he heard that word, although I can't be sure if he remembers where. One afternoon a few weeks ago our piano playing was interrupted by a commotion outside. Abandoning the Bechstein, we went out on to the steps to see a young tapir squealing with fright and in the last stages of the chase. Behind it followed a band of Indians armed with spears and, on their heels, a scattering of my tappers brandishing machetes. It was a rare instance of the two normally incompatible groups hunting together, and it had arisen only because the chase had spilled from the forest into the bounds of the estate.

It was the spears, in the end, that dispatched the exhausted creature. The anti-coagulant of the *tiki uba* sap with which they were tipped had caused it to bleed to death, leaving a broken strand of scarlet across the landscape. For some mysterious reason it had headed towards the house, to expire within a few metres of the front door.

Writhing in its death throes, it seemed to stare fixedly, almost accusingly, in our direction.

Before I could stop him, Eduardo ran towards it and bent down, looking into its fast fading sight. I would have run after him, but something prevented me. Perhaps it was the knowledge that he needed this encounter, that he must come to terms with the cessation of life and finality of death.

As he huddled over the twitching tapir, one of the Indians stooped and, prodding a finger into the wound, daubed a smear of blood over the boy's forehead. Everyone laughed – the Indians, the *seringueíros* – so that, when Eduardo turned to seek my reaction, I too had to smile and add my approval to this impromptu rite of passage. Not to have done so would have bewildered and confused him.

'Dead,' I said. 'The tapir is dead.'

And now, in the forest clearing, I repeated the lesson, pointing from the survivor to the fallen trees. 'Old . . . dead. Old . . . dead.'

'Dead,' he whispered. 'Old . . . dead.'

I waited to see if he would make the further connection unaided, but he seemed to be struggling with the burden of it.

Joining my palms to support my inclined head as though in sleep, I said, 'Dead,' and then pointed again to my chest and back to the fallen trees. 'Dead.'

He stared at me for a moment in silence, his lips working but unable to pronounce the word again. Then he took my hand and turned to lead me from that disquieting place.

We found our way barred by a quartet of Indians wearing nothing but war-paint and aiming arrows at us.

Had we, I wondered, disturbed a site they held sacred? Was that why no lumberjacks had intruded here?

Only then did I recollect why the glade struck a chord in my memory. Some three – maybe four – years ago, certainly before Eduardo was born, I had stood here, looking down on the corpse of a young logger who came in search of brazil-nut trees. He had paid the price for his trespass with an arrow in his neck. I remembered too the pains I took to demonstrate to his employers, with the help of the local FUNAI agent, that the victim had intruded some distance into the Indian reserve, where only I and a few others have been granted right of access.

I held out my arms in peace, recognising at least two of the Indians at the same moment they recognised me. They had been among the hunting party that pursued the tapir. They lowered their arrows, not having expected to find us wandering their preserve. Like me, Eduardo was still as a statue, returning their stare in silence.

The Indians nodded and indicated that we were free to go.

They know that I am a marked man, for they come from the tribe I am honour-bound to avenge.

As we were leaving the clearing, I spotted our first butterfly. Glossy black with a brilliant blue bar across the wings. Not one I have ever noticed before.

I drew it to the attention of Eduardo, who cried out with pleasure.

We watched it feasting on an ugly clump of fungus thrusting through the scaling bark of one of the dead trees. The sight of such beauty and putrescence in symbiosis was strangely comforting. While we stood there observing, another butterfly of the precise same colouring fluttered down to join it, its presence tolerated by the first without any display of aggression.

The break in the canopy allows them to descend to the forest floor, perhaps affording the chance to observe varieties one would not ordinarily see.

What were they doing?

Scavenging?

I really must learn more about butterflies. I shall bring Ruth Golding here to tell me why they feast on decaying matter.

If the Indians find out who she is, and why she is here, they may be concerned that she will take me before they have exacted their own ritual retribution.

How strange if the careful and patient investigations of Jewish Intelligence are undone, in the closing chapter, by the fulfilment of a pledge to a tribe of naked savages.

LIEBESLIEDER

I

I am haunted by the image of the butterfly and the fungus. That a creature so ephemeral should find sustenance in the product of something so old and rotten. Fleeting youth drawing upon the distilled essence of age. I find it almost unbearably moving.

As if, in spite of everything, I yet have some purpose to serve. Is it, after all, the education of Eduardo?

Or something else, still to be revealed?

Either way, I feel new vigour and energy coursing through this tired carcass. I want to be out and about. Not playing ancient tunes on a piano or listening to the music in my head as I watch the changing colours of the leaves.

I returned to O Varayo this morning and sought out Ruth Golding, who was in her hotel room, preparing her gear for a field excursion.

'I have found the perfect place for you,' I said. 'A clearing where the butterflies come down from the treetops, so close you can touch them.'

She seemed surprised. 'I didn't realise you were interested in butterflies?'

'I wasn't. Till you arrived.'

My directness took her aback. She almost blushed.

'Come with me and I will show you,' I said.

She hadn't expected her quarry to take the initiative, but it might reveal her hand if she were to decline my overture. She is, after all, a stranger in this land, and I can provide her with the means to add to the camouflage she has chosen to adopt. Also, familiarity might cause me to lower my guard and reveal more than I would do otherwise. After all, isn't that the choice stratagem of the investigator?

But I was obliged to warn her that I would be taking her into the Indian reserve, where she would be safe only in my company.

She asked why, and I explained that I was among the few who had won the confidence of the tribals in our area. Because, more than once, I have taken their side in disputes over boundaries and the dubious claims of settlers.

Given this proviso, she accepted my invitation. And with us came Eduardo.

I was curious to see how she would react to the boy, but she seemed entirely at ease with him, as if it were the most natural thing in the world that an Indian child should accompany a septuagenarian planter on a ramble through the rain forest in search of butterflies.

Perhaps it is her New York upbringing. They seem to be such a miscellany there.

I asked why – other than the pistol – she had brought only her camera and notebook. Where were her net, her killing jars and the swabs of chloroform I associated with her pursuit?

She said genuine lepidopterists hardly ever carried the implements with which to kill the objects of their research. Such articles were left to the 'collectors' who were endangering the rarer species.

It clashed with the image I had formed of her.

'Not even "bring 'em back alive"?' I asked.

She shook her head. 'Not unless we want them for breeding laboratory cultures.'

While we walked, I pointed out the different varieties of tree I had learned to identify, and all the time I was wondering why they had chosen her. Why not someone from the Zionist heartland? Some hand-picked, carefully trained manhunter from Jerusalem or Tel Aviv?

But perhaps that would be too obvious. The Americanness of Jews in New York can lead you to forget who they really are.

We reached the clearing, where I looked for the tree with the fungus. It was Eduardo who pointed it out. His eyes are keener. And sure enough the butterflies were there. Up to three of them hovering at any one time.

There was no sign of the Indians. If they were around they remained concealed.

She took the camera from her neck and carefully, quietly, screwed in a telephoto lens, her eyes fixed all the time on the dancing insects. Taking our cue from her stealthy movements, Eduardo slowly descended to a squatting posture while I gently lowered my buttocks on to a tree trunk a few metres away.

She took frame after frame, releasing the trigger tenderly, winding on the film by hand and lining up the viewfinder again with infinite care.

She clearly knew what she was doing.

When she had seen enough to discard the need for caution, she lowered the camera and turned to me.

'Do you know what they are?'

'Of course not. That's why I asked you here.'

I forget now the name she gave me. It doesn't matter. What does matter is that she knew. I am certain of that.

How long had she been doing this? I asked.

Since she had worked in Malaysia as a consultant architect to a project aided by funds from the World Bank.

I couldn't keep the note of exclamation from my voice. A consultant architect!

She shot me a look as if to ask how long I had buried myself in this jungle. As if my kind of chauvinism was a vanished phenomenon in the civilised world.

I wanted to ask what a good Jewish girl like her had been doing in a Muslim country, but thought better of it. She was, after all, a citizen of the United States. A full-blooded American Jewess.

Why shouldn't the world be her oyster?

I tactfully pursued the line of enquiry. Why the switch from architecture to lepidoptery?

It began when a friend of hers in the US Army Medical Research Unit, based in Kuala Lumpur, took her up into the Genting forest reserve to spend a day on an observation platform he had constructed in the tree canopy, specially to study the rich varieties of bird, animal and insect that abounded in the upper levels of virgin jungle, many of which would never be found at lower depths.

'It was wonderful,' she said. 'I fell in love with it. Like riding a raft on an ocean of greenery untouched by the prow of any ship. Discovering a richness of life all around that I never knew existed.'

'Isn't that from a line of poetry?' I asked, genuinely believing I had heard or read it somewhere.

If it was she wasn't aware of it.

'Do you realise,' she said, 'that the Malaysian rain forests are the oldest in the world? Much older than this. They formed part of the Sunda land mass, undisturbed for millennia. The species that evolved there have a few million years' head start over anything on this continent.'

I said nothing, watching her. And seeing too how Eduardo appeared equally mesmerised by her.

She reached her arms behind her to support her weight on the trunk she occupied, inclining her head backwards to follow the soaring grandeur of the solitary mahogany.

'Why do you suppose that tree is standing all alone?' she asked.

'I have no idea. Because it outlived all the others?'

She nodded.

'Big,' said Eduardo, showing off his vocabulary.

'Old,' I reminded him.

'Dead,' he added sadly.

She turned to him in surprise, and laughed. Which accentuated her beauty in a way that caught at my throat.

'Not yet,' she chided the boy. 'One day, maybe. And perhaps in your lifetime. But not yet.'

He looked from her to me, smiling with relief and shaking his head as if to say I told you so.

I wanted to reach out and touch her hair. To pull her gently down into the humus, where we would lie with our ears to the ground, listening to the muffled heartbeat of our great and ancient planet.

I couldn't think of a better place to die.

And yet she has awakened in me the will to live!

So late.
So pointlessly.

2

I am in love!

With the woman who has been sent to deliver me to judgement!

And the absurdity of it increases with each passing day.

I am becoming a source of embarrassment to her. I can't leave her alone. Feigning an interest in her work, which is only partly untrue, I beg to accompany her on her expeditions, pointing out that she has provided the only diversion I have known in years.

That I am old, slow and clearly incapable of being hauled up on ropes into forest canopies should the need arise is not, for her, the only problem. How is she to observe me if I spend all my time observing her?

I appreciate her difficulty, but it is quite beyond me to leave her in peace.

I am no better than a lovesick teenager, hopelessly fawning, ridiculously libidinous. I want to touch her, smell her, be as close to her as the bounds of our relationship will permit.

So far I have got away with it. Perhaps because I strike a comic note, play the part of the harmless, because elderly, satyr, sequestered too long in his lonely glade with just a faun of an Indian child for company.

She good-humouredly goes along with this, permitting both of us to accompany her on her forays, sometimes by water, but mostly on foot through narrow jungle trails laid down by free-roaming *seringueiros* or by secretive Indians who, on first detecting our approach, step aside from the trail, so that we are unaware of their presence until we are almost past them.

I have shown her, on the map she carries in her rucksack, the boundaries of the Indian reserve, cautioning her never to enter their vicinity without me to act as her escort. I am not sure if she believes me. I hope, for her sake, that she does.

She finds it disconcerting that the Indians never respond to her greeting.

'Why should they want you to "have a nice day"?' I ask her. 'Years of treachery from strangers have taught them to be always on their guard.'

She asks if we are in any danger from them outside their reserve and I reply, 'Of course! Did you forget your revolver?'

She corrects me. 'My pistol,' she says. And she hasn't forgotten it. She never does. But she is careful to conceal it in what is ostensibly her camera case. And it is quite clear that she knows how to use it.

Eduardo, who had been dying to test her prowess, asked her to shoot at a young anaconda looping from a branch beside a stream we were negotiating. She asked him why, since it wasn't harming him.

He shrugged. He is just a boy. And little boys are born with the impulse to destroy even before they know what it means to die. He is also an Indian, with the hunting instinct in his blood.

No, she said. She wouldn't shoot the anaconda. But she would shoot the branch supporting it.

And she did. From ten yards, bringing the startled reptile down into the stream, where it wisely sank from sight.

'Where did you learn to do that?' I asked.

'My pistol club in New York. I try and keep in practice.'

Eduardo was intrigued. Were there snakes in New York?

'Yes, but not the kind you find here,' she told him.

Much of what she finds here requires some getting used to. Though they may be the oldest in the world, the Malaysian rain forests haven't prepared her for the parasites that infest the jungles of Brazil.

Plagued by chiggers and mosquitoes in Manáus, she has been forewarned about sleeping without a light in native huts, where a far worse insect bite, from a lurking *barbeiro*, may implant a parasite that works its way through the body for years.

'Brazil,' I said, 'is full of old wives' tales which are largely untrue. Because few of the old wives survived to tell them.'

'What was the worst thing that ever happened to you?' she asked.

I thought about that.

'Nothing I have encountered in this country qualifies for that description,' I said.
She weighed my reply, looking deep into my eyes.
She knew exactly what I meant.
But I like playing these games.
Cat and mouse.
Surely it is permitted for the mouse to have some fun too?

3

Something very disturbing happened this afternoon, catching me completely unprepared.
And it should not have done. I should have anticipated it. Been prepared for it.
We were drinking in my favourite saloon. The one whose cracked floorboards now sag over the dried-up bed where the river once ran.
There were a few others present, including a group gambling in the corner furthest from the door.
One of my *seringueiros* approached and bent to whisper in my ear, telling me that the gambler with his back to the wall was the one who killed and buried the Indian girl in the smallholdings. The one I am pledged to hand over to the tribe.
I tried to take this in. Why was he still here? What the hell was he doing? What reason was there for him to keep returning?
I turned slowly, casually, to find that the man whose position had been described to me was staring back insolently, a half-smile playing on his lips. I wondered if he had put the tapper up to it, telling him to inform me of his presence, daring me to challenge him. His eyes were red, his cheeks hollowed, as if he were living on booze and cocaine.
I was glad that this time I had not brought Eduardo with me.
Ruth became aware that my gaze was fixed on a point across the room. She swung her head to find out why.
The opportunity for braggadochio was irresistible. The man staggered to his feet and lurched over to our table.

'You want me, Senhór?' he leered, leaning on his knuckles. 'Well here I am. What you going to do about it?'

I got to my feet, so angry I wanted to hit him. My heart was hammering beneath my ribs.

He moved surprisingly fast for one who had seemed inebriated and incapable. Sliding behind Ruth's chair, he hooked his left arm under her neck, hauling her upright and kicking the chair aside while with his right arm he jabbed a knife against her side.

I heard the scraping of other chairs as fellow patrons scuttled out of range. O Varayo is not used to such scenes.

We stood in a tableau of impending tragedy. I felt totally weak and helpless, knowing it was my own ineptitude and indecision that had placed her life at risk. The man's smile spread slowly, like the gape of a Halloween pumpkin.

Ruth remained perfectly still, but she spoke, choosing her words carefully.

'The camera case,' she said.

Seeing the bewilderment in my eyes, she repeated the sentence slowly, elaborating. 'The camera case . . . is on the chair beside you.'

But even if I had reacted it would not have been fast enough.

He released her and stepped back, replacing the knife in his belt and smoothing his soiled cuffs, the smile never leaving his face. Then he turned and walked slowly out of the door.

Ruth stood looking at me, her eyes widening with rage. She came round to my side of the table and grabbed at the case, which fell to the floor.

'Damn,' she said quietly, bending down to wrestle with the clasp. Removing the pistol, she ran outside.

The men who had retired into the corners of the saloon now cowered against the walls. One put his fingers to his ears and squeezed his eyes shut.

I heard her shouting, standing out in the narrow, rutted street and yelling at the top of her lungs. 'You bastard. Come out and face me like a man.'

I followed her, screwing up my face against the glare. There was no sign of the fellow. O Varayo had swallowed him without trace.

She turned to me and barked, 'Well? Aren't you going after him?'

'With what?'

'Here, take my gun.'

'I don't know how to use it. I have never used a gun.'

She stared at me incredulously, as if I had blundered from a Charlie Chaplin comedy on to the set of a Western.

'Who the hell was he?'

'One of the casual labourers who used to work on my estate.'

'What did he want with you?'

I shrugged. 'I don't know. Maybe he thought I hadn't paid him enough.'

She clearly couldn't accept that. 'I heard him say it was *you* who wanted *him*.'

'I can't imagine why.'

'What was that other man whispering in your ear?'

'He was simply warning me that the fellow was looking for trouble.'

Her mouth curled in disgust. 'Fat lot of use that was. He could have carried me off and you would have been left standing there.'

'You forget. I'm an old man. I don't move as fast as I used to.'

Her face softened. 'I'm sorry. It's just that I can't stand that kind of macho insolence. Had he still been in the street I would have put a bullet through him.'

'I believe you.'

And I did.

Especially if she had known why the Indians wanted him.

And how close she had come to eliminating the one rival claim on her chosen quarry.

SERENADE

I

Am I mistaken, or is she beginning to reflect towards me something of what I feel for her?

Am I so blind as to deceive myself? So old and foolish that I cannot recognise the hopelessness of my position?

Does she merely tolerate me, or do I detect the beginnings of genuine affection in her response?

It would be ironic if our constant proximity were subverting her very reason for coming. And wouldn't it also defeat my own purpose?

She is here, after all, to check me out, to verify the facts on record, to confirm the full weight of the evidence that piled up week after week, month after month, train after train.

Surely not all of them perished in the execution chambers? Surely some survived to point me out and say yes, I was the man they saw directing the traffic to the death camps? I was the one who gave the orders for the trains to depart?

It has happened already. In one show trial after another. The ancient accusers filing into the witness box, dredging up the harrowing, incriminating detail, breaking down with the unbearable burden of it. While the hardly less ancient accused sits stony faced, staring in front of him, shutting his mind behind iron gates to keep out the voices and the crowds. And the memories.

If I were in that seat I would nod my head and say yes, that *is* how it was. That *is* what happened.

If only I had the courage to make that journey unaided. To go alone and surrender myself to them. Why should I leave it to her to force my hand? As she must do in the end. Literally if necessary. But no, I am weak. I need my Nemesis to carry me there. I have waited for her so long that the river has all but dried up.

Time is running out. There are not many of us left to face our judgement, to remind the world of what we are, what we are capable of doing, what others might do in our place. For there are always others to follow in our footsteps. Yet now, more than ever, the world must be reminded, must be warned of the lengths to which people can go in obeying orders, in executing programmes, in blinding themselves to the realities of what they do in the name of progress.

Just as I must remind myself why she is here. And why, if I love her, it is for no other reason than the release she brings. The end to the waiting.

One cannot expect one's Nemesis to love in return. The Goddess of Vengeance? The punisher of transgressions? The bringer of retribution?

Yes, I am indeed a foolish old man.

Yet hope, they say, springs eternal. Even from the stone that has never cracked to admit it.

Perhaps it is possible for her to love, and yet still deliver me. Maybe to the extent that, when the time comes, she cannot bring herself to accompany me to that terrible court of world opinion, in the full glare of the spotlights and the television cameras. Instead when we are alone, in some secret corner of the forest that only the Indians visit, she will find the right moment, in the midst of discussing the butterflies or the nature of the universe, to pull the trigger when I least expect it, bringing it to a merciful, painless end.

If I can get her to love me that much!

The challenge it presents!

2

Why doesn't she question me?

Surely she must break down the façade of what I claim to be, and replace it with the patiently restored mosaic of what I was?

When will she begin?

She shows no sign of hurrying, no anxiety to complete what she has come to do. And she displays no curiosity whatsoever.

As if she knows all the answers already. So that there is no point in asking the questions.

Perhaps I am right. This is a subtle psychological ploy, to build up my confidence to the point where she will learn without having to ask. Allowing me to trust her so much I will begin to confide my innermost secrets, glad of the chance to unburden myself.

One cannot know all the tricks they employ these days.

This afternoon our route back to the house took us past Imelda's grave, in the old flower garden where Estancia does her best to keep the weeds at bay.

Recognising it for what it is, she paused, her raised eyebrow inviting an explanation.

'My wife,' I said.

She crouched to touch the lichened stonework where the simple legend is now all but obscured.

'How old was she?'

'Twenty-two.'

'So young?' She shook her head slowly. 'How did she die?'

'In childbirth. There was no doctor who could get here in time.'

She looked up. 'Your only child?'

'He would have been, yes.'

She turned to Eduardo, who had squatted beside her, staring at the stone.

'Dead,' said Eduardo.

She bit her lip and nodded, reaching out to touch his face. She looked up at me, her eyes telling me that she understands what Eduardo means to me.

She seemed genuinely moved.

By that one death!

Perhaps because it was something apart. Something of which she had received no prior information, revealing a side of me for which she was unprepared.

One tombstone cannot pay for all those other deaths, but it marks the simple, ordinary tragedy we must all face in our time. Maybe she had not expected to find that in me; the capacity to feel and to suffer as others feel and suffer.

In some respects these delaying tactics may be bringing her closer than she would wish to come, showing her more of me than she has any need to see.

And I have no wish to hurry her.

Each new day with her is a reprieve, a stay of execution, another step on a journey I am amazed to find myself making so late in my life.

3

Father Lorenzo is more than a little shocked by my behaviour. I am, after all, old enough to be her grandfather. And it is common knowledge in O Varayo that I am besotted by her.

Seeing me hurrying along the bank of the canal in the twilight, wearing my best suit for dinner at the Trocadero, my tappers smile knowingly and wink at each other. '*Ôba, Patróno!*' they call out through the anonymity of darkness. Where am I off to so late in the evening? What business do I have in O Varayo that is so pressing?

Their laughter follows me down the cutting.

I do not mind if it amuses them that a harmless old goat like me, who has lived so silently all these years, should suddenly drop a fully inflated scrotum where all can see, and go charging about his pasture with an appetite for more than grazing.

As long as she doesn't see me that way.

It doesn't even matter that Father Lorenzo lectures me on the subject. I am obliged to be patient with him. All these years I have denied him the prize of my salvation. Surely, having been the cause of so much disappointment, I owe him this opportunity to rebuke me for my morals?

And he does, quite comprehensively, pointing out the difference in our ages and backgrounds, the way I am shamelessly throwing myself at her.

He spares me nothing, warming to his admonitions, laying them on with the vigour of a Roman centurion applying the lash. He would have made a good prosecutor for the Spanish Inquisition, and I can see, at times, that this worries him. He tries hard to balance his sermons, to strike a compromise between punishment and love. When he delivers them from the pulpit, they end up sounding all fire and molasses, leaving his parishioners confused as to whether they have been castigated or forgiven.

I know this even without attending his Mass, for Esquamillo reports it to me with much affectionate mimicry, while Estancia scowls at him and retires to the kitchen to remove her shawl and prepare a late breakfast.

And so I allow the good Father to scold me and to pray for me. For I know that he does pray. That years of entreaties have been wasted upon me. Delivered up from the silence of his little room behind the chapel where the rosaries hang and smoke-grimed holy pictures, peeling from age but never neglect, plaster the walls.

The courage of his prayer! To rise from that little circle of flickering light and attempt the impossible journey from this immensity of darkened wilderness!

I envy him his faith!

But I left myself on the canal bank, hurrying towards my tryst at the Trocadero, where she is waiting for me in a dress I have seen a dozen times but which still looks fresh upon her, perfect for the candlelight and the scent of jasmine through the open window.

The Trocadero is transformed. A barn converted into a theatre for a one time only, never to be repeated engagement of a touring performer whose likes have seldom been seen so far upriver. Remedios has not done such business in all the years since he opened this dosshouse. He and his wife spend their time acquiring culinary skills they had no thought of ever possessing. They spurn the one remaining provision store and send to Paromante for their supplies!

Every evening Ruth holds court in the dining room, and buys drinks for those who will come and identify, from the Polaroids she has taken for reference purposes, the new species we have discovered. Even if she knows the scientific labels, she wants to note down the local terms.

Many of which have never existed until now, for I am sure more than half the men who are so readily volunteering their services are inventing the names for the pleasure of joining her, however briefly, at her table.

It isn't even the drinks she buys them. They have their minds set on how they can get her to bed, and they use all their crudely undeveloped charms to that end, causing her to shake a disapproving finger but also sometimes to laugh at their bold innuendo.

It worries Senhóra Remedios that she allows these familiarities, and it worries me too.

But were I to admit that to her I know she would only smile indulgently. After all, who am I to talk? What is it that I want from her? And do I imagine she is incapable of looking after herself?

Instead I content myself with the knowledge that, when the interviews are completed, and the volunteers have no further information to add, it is I who stay for dinner while they return to their wives and families.

There are few other distractions in O Varayo. Ever since the ugly incident with the billigerent peon who held a knife to her side, she declines to drink at the saloon, and there is not, nor has there ever been, a cinema.

So all that is left to us, aside from dinner, is a walk before the light fades along the river bank to the football field.

It amuses her to see how seriously we regard the sport. She is less concerned with what happens on the pitch than with the frenzy of the spectators.

'*Ôba*, Roberto,' they cry. 'Give it to him good! Go for his balls! Step on his face! Please, Manuel, don't let go of it. You bandit! You monkey brain! Just wait till after the game!'

Aware of our presence, they pause to smile and nod courteously before all their attention returns to the ball. 'Get out of the way, piranha meat! You swallower of snakes! Go fuck an Indian!'

'As bad as any baseball game in the Bronx!' says Ruth. 'And for me just as incomprehensible.'

'It's all about domination.'

'Not so much in order to win as to do the other man down!'

'Oh, don't worry about them. When the game is over they will go off arm in arm, laughing at the goals they missed. It's your civilised man you have to worry about. The higher the stakes, the greater the aggression.'

She looks at me with an expression I can't quite distinguish in the waning light. 'You sound as if you speak from experience.'

'I do. That is what brought me here.'

She shrugs. 'It wouldn't be enough to keep me here.'

And she lets the ball drop! Just like that! As if it isn't worth running with because she knows already where it will lead.

What am I to make of her?

4

Over dinner tonight she suddenly said, 'I have a confession to make.'

I lifted my napkin and carefully wiped my mouth, preparing myself for the revelation I had been expecting, sorry only that she would deliver it in the midst of our meal, in the glow of the candlelight.

'I told you,' she said, 'that I took up my occupation only when I got to Malaysia, almost as if I stumbled across it by chance. That is not strictly true. I had been running away from it.'

'From collecting butterflies?'

She nodded. 'I come from a family of naturalists. I tried hard to break with that tradition.'

'By becoming an architect?'

'Yes, but it wasn't that easy. When I was up there in that tree I felt the old urge come over me. To escape from the office, from the drawing board, and return to the fields and the forests. It's a strange thing. All of my family are infected with this impulse. It's almost a curse.'

'A nice thing to be cursed with, if you happen to attract the malignance of some jealous divinity. But a strange fate for a family of Jews.'

'I know. We don't really fit the mould. We should have been bankers and moneylenders. That's the popular stereotype, isn't it?'

Why was she telling me this? Apart from that first day we met, when I was overcome with curiosity, I have avoided asking her questions, just as she has refrained from putting hers to me. I didn't want to break the spell that was slowly settling upon me.

'We emigrated to the States in the thirties,' she said. 'My grandfather had been one of Poland's most eminent professors of natural history.'

Poland! So soon before the holocaust!

'He was offered a professorship at Harvard. I was born in New York, where my father was attached to the American Museum of Natural History. Do you know it?'

'I've heard of it.'

'When I was still a child he took me with him, collecting specimens in the field. The smaller mammals mostly. But in territory where we were vulnerable to the larger ones. In Africa we learned always to keep within range of the trees, in case we were charged by rhino. I felt at home in the branches, and the higher I climbed, of course, the further I could see.'

I shook my head. 'I have never felt comfortable in trees. I have no head for heights.'

'You don't know what you're missing. It's never too late to learn. I have – or perhaps I should say had – two uncles, both of whom also followed the trail my grandfather blazed. One of them is still alive.'

'And the other?'

'His speciality was vultures. And his greatest love the condor, one of the few scavengers that also kill their prey. After he died, my father received his notebook. It had been found beside his remains at the foot of a ravine in the Andes. From the last entry it was clear he was still alive and conscious after the fall. He had slipped from a ledge on his way to investigate an eyrie. His hip was shattered, and he knew he would never get out alive. The condors had found him. Two of them.'

She paused, and I could see it was an effort for her to continue. I refilled her glass.

'He wrote, "It has been a hard winter for them. The game has been scarce. I sense they are too hungry to wait. I am only glad that my death will save them."'

She put the glass to her lips and drank.

I said nothing. I wanted her to go on. To explain the point of this story. Was it offered as a parable of my own condition?

'I was still in my teens when he died. I had been close to him. We were a close family, always getting together, when we returned from our travels, to compare notes. Which is why he had scribbled in his log a message asking the finder to send it to my father. I thought no, I cannot do this. Animals are beautiful, yes, but they are not worth dying for. So I chose architecture as a career.'

'Until you discovered that butterflies don't kill you?'

She smiled. 'Not butterflies, no. Unlike mosquitoes, they don't even carry killer diseases.'

'Have you worked with other insects?'

'My friend in Malaysia, the one who built the observation platform, was a specialist in malaria vectors. He had perfected a way to breed *anopheles meticulatus* in laboratory conditions. It's a mosquito with a hang-up. No amount of encouragement will persuade it to breed in a synthetic environment. It opts for sterility rather than surrender its secrets.'

'How did your friend overcome its reticence?'

'He would sedate a row of females and lay them on their backs. Then he would lower upon them a freshly beheaded male. With the mental block removed, instinct took over. One male could impregnate up to seven females in quick succession before it died.'

'Charming.'

'I prefer butterflies.'

'I'm glad to hear it.'

Cat and mouse. I'm now more than ever convinced of it. But how long can we keep this up?

TOTENTANZ

I

I am suffering nightmares.
Real nightmares.
In my sleep!
I had not thought it possible I could dream anything worse than is already locked in my waking mind.
Yet it is.
One night last week I was standing in the goods yard, watching – and not watching – the silent stream endlessly shuffling past, when something possessed me to look into their faces.
They were all women. And they all had the same face.
Her face.
They returned my stare. Not accusing. Not despairing.
Just bewildered as to why I was there. Why I was doing this.
I was struck immobile, unable to move. Incapable of finding the answer. For them. Even for myself.
I had known that answer once. Had used it repeatedly to defend my presence alongside that river of humanity. But it would not come to me. I could find no word to explain my role there.
What *was* I doing there?
Observing?
No. Much more.
I was there to *re-route* the river. To divert it from the mainstream of life and send it to another destination, far out of sight,

where it would sink without trace, never to reach its distant goal.

No, no, I cried out in my sleep. There was a word for it.

And I awoke with the cry still on my lips, remembering the word instantly.

Duty.

Two nights ago I was in the signal box, with the levers under my hand. The phone rang and a voice I did not recognise said, 'Clear the line, clear the line! The Führer is coming.'

The line was full of people. I could see that. There was no way I could clear it in time. I was unable to give the order, unable to speak.

I looked down into that seething mass of people and I saw her face staring back at me. She had fallen on the rails, unable to rise. She was lying on the main track, and the train was coming. I could see the distant smoke of it smudging the horizon, approaching as fast as a thundercloud.

I had my hand on the levers. I could divert the train to its destruction in the siding, or I could let it run on.

I was the Station Master. The only one who could do this.

And still I couldn't move!

Her face looked back at me, not pleading, not asking for anything.

Just waiting to see what I would do.

Last night the dream was worse.

I was lying in bed, my arms around her.

And she looked back at me with infinite pity. With the look I have longed to see just once before I die.

Even if only in the eyes of my executioner.

She returned my love, holding me close.

And I heard again the music of Franz Liszt. Something I have not heard in years.

The *Consolations*, just as Rachel played them. Softly, barely impinging on the ear, but penetrating to the heart.

She looked at me and whispered, 'Do you remember Rachel?'

I made myself remember, and I said, 'Yes.'

'She sent me to thank you for saving her.'

'Saving her?' My heart leapt. 'She is safe then?'

She nodded. 'The train never got there. Rachel is in New York.'

'Thank God,' I murmured. 'Thank God.'

I hugged her with relief, as if it *were* Rachel lying there in her place.

And then the question occurred to me. 'Who are you? What are you to Rachel?'

'I am her daughter. I am your child.'

Even awake, the nightmare lingered. It was so real. The texture of the sheets. Every detail of the room. Every bar of music, just as I had remembered.

The *Consolations*!

There was a time when my dreams were my only consolations, rearranging my memories to purge the reality and replace it with more acceptable alternatives.

What is happening to me?

Maybe that is why Ruth is here.

Not to take me back to trial, to mass exposure in the world press, to the ignominy of facing those of my accusers who still survive (for I cannot have outlived them all).

But to compel me, by her mere presence, to remember.

To accuse myself. To condemn myself. To suffer my own death at my own hands. Because, once I have forced myself to look into each of those faces shuffling past in the stream, the dream and the reality will become one. And there will be no further escape, even in my sleep. So that I can no longer bear the whole terrible burden of the truth.

This is not how I wanted it to end.

I must confront her, have it out with her, make her reveal her reason for coming. So that she will have no alternative but to take the responsibility for it.

And yet to do so would be to destroy all that this relationship has meant to me. By tearing away whatever pretence she maintains in order to reveal that she has no feeling for me at all. That she is here only for what she has to do.

Driven by her own sense of duty.

2

Time is running out.

She told me today that she would be leaving soon, that she has gathered as much data as this region can yield and that she must return to New York to put it all into the computer.

She may come back some day to carry on her research, but if so not in 'this neck of the woods'.

Can she be serious?

Or is she testing me, to see how I will react?

What does she expect me to betray? Relief? Dismay? Or no emotion at all except, 'Fine. And be sure to have a nice day.'

Maybe she will save it to the last, to give me every opportunity to crack.

I won't give her that pleasure. I won't go down on my knees before her in a mumbling, stuttering travesty of confession.

Hers are the faces I now see nightly in my dreams. Always looking to me for answers, never putting the questions.

What do they expect of me?

I didn't create my circumstances. I didn't ask to be put in charge of that station at that point in time. The war changed everything. We were all made to do things we wouldn't ordinarily choose to do.

Duty! Duty!

Doesn't anyone understand that word any more?

Doesn't anyone know the power it can unleash?

So when she told me I just looked back at her and said nothing.

Why should it be me who has to supply the answers?

It is now her world.

What we did with it, so long ago, is barely of academic interest. For historians only. What lessons it could teach would now fall on deaf ears.

Already, even in Germany, the cycle is starting again. Neo-Nazism they call it. Like a new brand of washing powder. And somehow the fear that word could instil is watered down. Nobody believes it any more. A fringe, crackpot obsession for those fanatics who always dwell in the shadows of society. And in this under-estimation lies their hope and their future strength. For they can insinuate themselves again in ever more prominent positions, barely noticed until, like a plague of cockroaches, they erupt through the walls and the floorboards and take possession of the house.

My appearance in court would serve only to reinforce the unreality of that threat. Like a petrified mummy, exhumed from the past, I would be exhibited and analysed alongside the others of my vintage. Look what these men did! And listen to those still alive to tell it!

Tell it to whom?
Who would believe?
Who would care?
It was all so long ago.

And the descendants of those who suffered are now usurping the lands they have seized from others. Driving Arab schoolchildren to throw stones at them. Let he who casts the first stone receive the first bullet!

Lebensraum!
Living room.
Go, Ruth. Go back. Leave me to my music room.
And take the world with you when you leave.

3

Yet, despite her declaration that her work is nearing an end, she is not ready to leave. She makes excuses to stay. She has not found the opportunity, she says, to make use of the climbing gear. Her choice is narrowing down to a few promising sectors of jungle where she expects the canopy to yield the best results.

Her goal is the thick, undisturbed 'gallery forests', with upper branches firm enough to provide a roost for her observations, yet bearing foliage sufficiently sparse to afford good views on all sides.

'Does this run in the family too?' I ask. 'This obsession with climbing trees?'

'Not for its own sake. Only where it helps our research. My Uncle Gus had a strange assignment once. He's the other uncle. The one who's still alive. He was invited by the Indian government to advise on the conservation of the white rhino. While he was out there, an elephant bearing a party of tourists through a game reserve was spooked by a tiger.'

She seemed to find it difficult keeping a straight face, so I expected something amusing.

'I shouldn't laugh,' she said. 'It isn't funny really. A lot of people got hurt. And they were old people. Retired American couples doing something different. Something with just a touch of adventure and yet nothing – they thought – too dangerous. Fortunately no one was killed.'

'So what happened?'

'The elephant ran for miles. The mahout was among the first to be thrown. Then the howdah slipped to one side, and that's when the rest of them had to make their choices. Whether to jump or hang on. In the end they all fell, most of them scraped off by the trees. Uncle Gus followed in a Land Rover. It was like a paper chase, except that the trail consisted of smashed cameras, broken parasols and little old ladies draped over branches.'

I laughed politely, but she was right. It wasn't funny really.

'What happened to the tiger? Did he get there first to pick up the pieces?'

'Fortunately, no. The tiger disappeared, probably more frightened than the elephant. The biggest problem for Uncle Gus was collecting them all and lowering them from the trees so that they could be delivered to hospital without further damage to fractured limbs and broken bones. Then the tour company's insurance investigator arrived on the scene. And boy did he have trouble trying to determine liability! Who was responsible? The government, the game warden, the mahout, the elephant or the tiger? Or even, God forbid, the tour company?'

'What was the decision?'

'My uncle never stayed to find out.'

Again these parables, these allegories!

What does she hope to achieve? Is this a war of nerves?

CARNAVAL DES ANIMAUX

I

She reels off the names of threatened animal species as if she were listing stock depreciating in a bear market. And Brazil, she says, is where the danger is gravest, where their natural habitats are disappearing faster, and with the most sweeping consequences.

Why then, I ask, does she spend her time cataloguing butterflies when there are so many larger, rarer species heading for extinction?

Butterflies, she points out, are also on the 'hit list'. The toll from a single forest fire – and the jungle is being burned off at the rate of thousands of hectares each day – is prodigious. If they are not consumed instantly in the heat, the fragile wings of lepidoptera can scorch and wither in the updraft, hundreds of metres above the trees. The purpose of her sojourn in this country is not a leisurely ramble with a camera to take in form and colour but to check out the areas suffering the greatest loss.

Here? Even here?

Soon maybe, but not yet. So far her log shows that we are better off than most other regions. Her spot census is revealing greater concentrations of the common species, which suggests that those which elsewhere are more scarce, because less adaptable, are also surviving reasonably well here. This could almost serve as a barometer against which to measure the depredations in other areas.

And what about other varieties of wild life? Are they faring well in this 'neck of the woods'?

From what she knows, and what she has seen of them, it would appear so.

I inform her that in all my years here I have never seen a jaguar, never heard its voice.

That doesn't mean, she remarks, that it isn't there. Only that I am a poor observer, not trained to see the marks where its claws have scratched the bark.

She lends me the only book she carries in her rucksack, other than her notebooks and reference manuals. Entitled *Tukani*, it is written by Dr Helmut Sick, formerly an ornithologist at the University of Berlin. She draws a passage to my attention.

He writes:

One day, quite unexpectedly, I found myself face to face with a female puma. She was a few yards in front of me in the depth of the forest and I did not, at first, realize the fact. My attention had been attracted by a flicker of yellow in the green foliage. Nature has given the puma a skin of one single colour and the alternating deep shadow and little patches of sunlight had turned it into a mosaic which seemed ... to be covered with a camouflage net – a camouflage, incidentally, that the spotted jaguar, who is much more of a forest-dweller, possesses as part and parcel of his normal equipment. The puma in front of me remained absolutely motionless. While I was still admiring the play of light and shade in the deep forest, something stirred on the ground, and a baby puma emerged; it wriggled out and squatted in front of its mother! Although these great beasts of prey will normally flee at the slightest noise, there are two situations in which they are really dangerous – when they are cornered and when they have their young with them ... I began to withdraw just as cautiously as I had previously advanced. The puma never moved. I was probably the first human being she had ever seen.

Reading this passage again in the quiet of the music room, I am struck by the accident of history which stranded my fellow countryman in the Brazilian jungle at the outbreak of the war.

Interned as an enemy alien, Dr Sick was invited, when hostilities ceased, to join the staff of the Museo Nacional in Rio.

The museum in Berlin had sent him to this country on a collecting expedition but, following his release from incarceration, he stayed on to survey a route through the states of Mato Grosso and Para to the Amazon. Like Darwin, the lone naturalist on a voyage to map the world and make it more accessible, Dr Sick conducted his research in the company of road builders and engineers.

2

I ask her this morning why she has narrowed down her choice of reading material to just this one work. Why a German? Why not an American?

She professes not to understand the question. What does nationality have to do with it? It so happens that Helmut Sick was one of the first to open the eyes of the world to the fate of plant and animal life in Brazil if indiscriminate land development were to continue unchecked. He also appealed for the creation of special reserves to save the Indians from the same threat of extinction.

Opposition, she says, came not only from business and real-estate interests but also from the Church, which, given the choice, would rather collect a tally of Indian souls, delivered up on their death beds if necessary, than see them live on in ignorance of God.

Oddly enough, I tell her, I believe Father Lorenzo would agree with her.

She points out that last year alone Brazil lost an area of tropical rain forest larger than Switzerland, the country from which I claim to originate. And also last year one of the leading crusaders against deforestation, Francisco Mendes, was murdered by cattle ranchers.

It would be understandable if this were a country suffering gross overpopulation, like India or Bangladesh, but Brazil has a low population density and plenty of good farmland. Why do settlers crowd into the Amazon, where the land is not suitable for agriculture and where farmers can barely maintain subsistence levels?

I point out that the legal and tax systems have made deforestation and ranching artificially profitable. The government's financial subsidies for livestock ranches over the past decade represent the biggest known subsidy in history for ecological destruction without economic gain.

There are other factors compounding this imbalance. High inflation has discouraged cash savings, so that everyone wants to invest in land. The government has virtually exempted agriculture from taxation, so that businessmen are encouraged to buy farmland and misdeclare their business profits as farm income. It doesn't matter to them that the treeless land sits empty, slowly eroding into desert, and that those genuine farmers they bought out have now headed deeper west to dispossess the Indians.

What about me, she asks. Am I profiting from subsidies and tax dispensations?

I point out that I took over an abandoned property, that I have done nothing to extend it but have concentrated only on developing it to its fullest potential. And when I arrived there were no incentives of the kind that are fuelling the current inroads into the hinterland.

'Where I saw injustice I did my best to prevent it,' I declare. 'In disputes between settlers and Indians I was frequently the one to arbitrate. The *cabóclos* and the *garimpeíros* may not love me, but they respect me.'

'Who are they?' she asks.

'The so-called frontiersmen and the prospectors. We are all one big fraternity of colonists here. It is only the Indians who don't belong.'

'And what were the results of your arbitration?'

'Frequently I found in favour of the Indians, and the settlers had to pack up and go back where they came from.'

'Just like that? With no opposition to your decree?'

'There is no law here. No policemen, no courts, no lawyers. It is still the land where the strong survive.'

'And you are the strong?'

'I represent stability, continuity and a sense of order, yes. That counts for something, even here.'

Her challenge of my principles puts me on the defensive, to the point where I begin to argue even for the ethos of the Brazilians. Why, I ask, should they be expected to administer their country as though it were a global rather than a national resource? Hasn't everyone else done exactly what the Brazilians are doing? Wasn't Europe the first to lose its forests?

She evades the question. 'How long after we are gone,' she counters, 'will it take this planet to recover from the wounds we have inflicted upon it?'

I shrug. 'Twenty years? Thirty years? We humans may prove of less consequence than we would like to think. Our architecture will remain, yes. Like taller, uglier, latter-day variants of Inca ruins mouldering in their creeping foliage. And extra-terrestrial visitors may decode our libraries and find sufficient evidence to determine how we died.'

'How? AIDS? Drugs? World War Three?'

'Through sheer incompetence. Mismanagement of the paradise God gave us. The prime property in the universe squandered on undesirable tenants.'

3

She tells me today that I have been giving Father Lorenzo a hard time.

'He has been complaining to you?'

'Less in anger than in sorrow.'

'It should be neither. He enjoys our theosophical debates. They enliven the tedium of his existence.'

'He finds them exhausting. You never let him win.'

'He is too modest. Tell him I relish the challenge he poses for me, and consider myself fortunate to be blessed with so formidable an adversary in so unlikely a setting.'

'You take pleasure, he says, in baiting him.'

I laugh. 'You should hear the things he says to me in return!

He never fails to remind me of the length of the spoon he must use to sup with me.'

She looks at me, levelly. 'Do you believe in God?'

'But certainly. The God of the Israelites, no less. The vengeful divinity biding his time to exact retribution.'

'That is not the God of the Israelites. Not all of Him, anyway. You have not read the Talmud.'

I come close to telling her that I have seen it often enough. Ancient, dog-eared copies of it, extracted like fingernails from the trembling hands of the elders, when it was the last thing they had but for the clothes they wore.

'Do you believe in heaven?' she probes.

'I believe in hell. I have a very vivid, very real picture of hell fixed in my mind. Hell is a railway station, where everyone else is departing for other destinations and I am the only one left behind.'

She registers no change in expression.

But then she never responds to these clues. She will settle for nothing but the full, absolute truth.

REQUIEM

I

How much has happened in these last three days! Where to begin?

It must be when she told me, two days ago, that she had found the perfect tree to make a start on her aerial observations. She had already carried out a trial ascent, and her equipment had coped very satisfactorily. She was hopeful that these upper galleries of foliage would present a much richer variety than we had found on the ground. All we had seen so far was what we had come across in the clearings, along the trails or on the river banks. She was sure there were other species up there which never come down to the forest floor, and she must check them out.

My old fear of heights came back to me, but my curiosity, and my desire to be near her, got the better of me. I could at least go along to help, even if I had to remain below. Perhaps she would need me down there if she wanted equipment hauled up to her?

She accepted the suggestion, but advised me not to bring Eduardo, who would only want to climb with her. She would not be able to give him her full attention until she had managed to get 'the feel of the ropes'.

Anyway, we would be starting well before dawn because she wanted to be up in position before the sun climbed above the tree line.

So that night I invented an excuse for Eduardo. I lied to him, telling him I would be in O Varayo all day on business.

Taking my best torch, I let myself out of the house at four in the morning, quietly, so as not to disturb Estancia, who would otherwise have insisted on getting up to make breakfast.

The night air was damp on my cheeks, and frogs flopped in the torchlight, seeking the shadows of the undergrowth. The bird I have never seen, which the Indians call the ghost bird because it haunts the sleepless and troubles the guilty, was still abroad, switching its low whistle from tree to unseen tree, like a grave robber keeping track of an accomplice.

I am not used to the forest at night. It is a strange, threatening place. Even the hat lamps of the early morning tappers, flitting like will-o'-the-wisps between the columns of rubber, seemed to follow me like the eyes of prowling animals.

When I arrived at the rendezvous, halfway along the canal, she was already there, with her equipment stacked in a pile at her feet. To get to the tree she had selected we would have to strike at right angles down the lines of rubber until we reached the cliffs of primary vegetation at the edge of the estate.

I carried the harness, the ropes and the metal clamps she fixes to them for climbing. She shouldered the rucksack containing the rest of the gear, together with her camera case, inside which, I felt sure, was the gun. She wore climbing boots and a helmet with a lamp she would use to illuminate her ascent.

We walked single file, she leading, purposeful, methodical, knowing exactly where she was going. Once we passed a pair of tappers still stripping thin slivers of bark to bleed the latex. They stopped in surprise to watch us as we passed, saying not a word.

She told me once she felt uncomfortable in man-made forests which were being slowly, scientifically drained of their sap. The wounded trunks, surgically incised each day and never allowed to heal, reminded her of experiments with animals.

Reaching the forest wall, she looked for and soon found the trail she had marked, following it into a blackness as deep and suffocating as a passage to a Pharaoh's burial chamber. If any life existed here it would be in the higher branches, closer to the air and the sunlight. Only the Indians used these paths, and their spears were for aiming upwards, at the creatures that flew and leapt and hung suspended from above. I understood for the first time why she had planned this from the outset as a climbing expedition.

We walked for perhaps twenty minutes. In the darkness, when we reached the tree she had targeted for climbing, I could see nothing to suggest why she had chosen this in preference to the others. But she had left evidence of her trial ascent. A rope dangled down the trunk. Somehow the silence discouraged conversation. Nor could I make any contribution, merely watching as she prepared her apparatus, conscious that I would remain useless to her unless she assigned me a supporting role.

She never once spoke. Never said, 'Hold this,' or 'Do that.' I might as well not have been there. And yet, just before she began her ascent, she turned to kiss me on the cheek.

I was stunned. What had impelled her to do it? We had not so much as held hands in all the time we had been together.

For how should the moth kiss the flame?

The first twelve metres of trunk were sheer, with nothing to offer a handhold. She sealed them by fixing clamps to the rope, alternately sliding these up and locking them to hold her weight, which, in addition to the harness, was borne by stirrups strapped to her boots and ankles. She climbed quickly, economically. I marvelled at how easy she made it seem.

Craning my head upwards to follow her, I soon developed a crick in my neck, which prompted me to seek out the roots of an adjacent tree, where I could sit and lean back for a better view. All I saw was a patch of light on the bark and the undefined silhouette of her body ascending higher and higher.

At about thirty metres she spoke, more to herself than to me, although her voice carried clearly down from the vaulted chambers of foliage.

'Damn,' she said, 'I'm going to miss the sunrise.'

She made it seem a tragedy, like missing the Resurrection.

By now she had climbed so high that the lamp was no longer visible. I was on my own on the forest floor, waiting for the jungle to awaken and wondering if it ever would.

I marvelled again at her professionalism, at the extraordinary competence she displayed in skills beyond the reach of many men I had known.

She had pointed out the description of the puma in Dr Sick's book. Though I could recall no reports of either pumas or jaguars in our locality, she had reminded me this was no reason to suppose they weren't here. And if they were, they and their prey could vanish without trace. Jaguars are climbers too. And she had the gun with her.

The palest haloes of light were forming in the canopy, like galaxies viewed across infinite voids of space, when suddenly I heard her voice, made almost celestial by distance, calling, 'Watch out below!' Followed by a crashing and tearing that brought me to my feet.

I saw what it was. The harness had fallen, together with the metal clamps, the stirrups and a spare rope, threshing and jerking like the coils of an endless anaconda.

My heart leapt. Was she in difficulties?

She had to shout to make herself heard, and even then it reached me only faintly. 'I've sent the harness down. Have you got it?'

I cupped my hands to my mouth and yelled back. 'It's here. What do you want me to do with it?'

'Put it on, together with the leg straps, and start climbing.'

It seemed there was the slightest of time lags, as if our voices were taking split seconds to reach each other.

'I can't,' I called. 'I'm afraid of heights.'

'Don't be silly. I've done all the work for you. All you have to do is strap yourself in and slide the clamps up the spare rope. You watched me do it. It's easy.'

I wished I had watched with greater attention. I held up the harness in disbelief. It bristled and jangled with clasps and buckles.

'I promise you,' her voice continued, 'that the rope is safely secured. I'll be taking some of the weight on the pulleys.'

Instantly my heart was thumping with the unexpectedness of it. So here it was! This was it!

The test! And still I couldn't bring myself to take it.

'I'm too old for this,' I cried.

'Don't be a sissy, Kristian. Just be careful not to get yourself entangled in the branches.'

By God I would do it! Or die trying.

I buckled on the stirrups, harnessed myself to the clamps and fixed them to the rope she had dropped for me. I found the clamps slipped easily up the nylon, but locked instantly when I pulled down on them.

'I'm coming!' I yelled.

2

'Remember,' she called, 'not to look down.'

And I didn't.

I looked only at the tree in front of me, surmounting metre after slow metre, occasionally planting my stirruped shoes against the calloused bark to stop myself swinging. The worst of it was negotiating the branches, which jutted out at all angles, each presenting a different set of hazards.

The rope itself was less of a problem than I had supposed, for she had tethered to the crown a complex system of pulleys to spread the load, and was hauling on this herself so that I wouldn't have to take all the burden.

Things progressed reasonably well until, at about thirty-five metres, I came up directly under the largest branch, almost a separate fork of the tree, across which the rope was inclined. When I negotiated this I found myself swinging out like a pendulum on the other side, twisting in the air well clear of the trunk.

I couldn't help myself. I cried out in panic.

'Get a hold of yourself, Kristian,' she commanded, her voice now only a few metres above me. 'You're perfectly safe. Just climb the rope.'

'I can't.'

'Just climb the rope, Kristian.'

'I'm spinning like a top.'

'Climb the rope.'

'I'm terrified.'

'The rope, Kristian. The rope.'

'Cut me free. Let me fall. I can't go on.'

'Damn you, Kristian.'

The rope jerked. She was taking the full load without my help. Slowly she reeled me in until I was sufficiently shamed by her to contribute my share.

At last she reached out her hand and helped me across the lip of the cup formed within the crown of the tree, which she had converted into her observation lair.

I was drenched in light, stunned to find how bright it was in contrast to the darkness through which I had climbed. I had the feeling we were suspended high above the surface of the planet.

Clinging to her, shaking and weeping like the helpless old man I am, I pulled her down with me into the bottom of that cradle in the sky, so that I wouldn't have to look back on the terrors I had survived.

'Thank you,' I sobbed. 'Thank you for not letting go.'

She held my head against her breast to comfort me. 'How could I have let go? What would I tell Eduardo?'

3

'You missed the dawn,' she said. 'It was wonderful.'

I raised my head and screwed up my eyes just long enough to squint at armadas of cirrus, still tinged with pink.

A breeze caught the sails of foliage and pushed us in a slow arc across the sky, like the mast of a great ship at sea.

I closed my eyes again and said, 'I'm going to be sick.'

'You'll get used to it. Just don't think about it.' She cupped her body closer to mine. 'Why were you so frightened?'

'I have always suffered from vertigo.'

'You asked me to cut you free. That's the last thing you would say if you were afraid of falling.'

'I thought it would save time. Spare me the agony.'

'Of what? Climbing down again?'

'Of ending this. Of you filing your report and me having at last to "face the music" as they say.'

'Filing what report? On butterflies? And what music would you have to face? I don't follow you.'

I twisted my head to look into her eyes. 'Isn't it time we stopped playing games?'

'You're the one who's playing them. I don't know what you're talking about.'

'You haven't come here to arrange my extradition?'

'Extradition? For God's sake, Kristian, start making sense or I'm going to toss you overboard to preserve my sanity. What the hell are you on about?'

She genuinely didn't know!

All that time she had been doing nothing but study butterflies. She had never heard of me until I introduced myself at the Trocadero.

But I had said too much to save myself now. I let it all come out, word by word, detail by detail, every last agonising memory of who I had been before I became who I was.

Up there in the sky, suspended halfway between heaven and hell, it didn't matter any longer if she knew, if the world knew. I was so sure of my inability to survive the descent that I could see no life for me beyond that. Only what had been. What had led to this moment, with Ruth beside me, listening to me pour out my soul.

I cried.

I could not stop crying.

A whole lifetime of tears gushed from me.

But she never said a word. Never stopped rocking me gently, stroking my hair, cradling me in her arms like a baby. Until I realised that was exactly what I was. As in the nursery rhyme.

My wellsprings of guilt running dry, I fell silent at last and waited for her to speak. When she still said nothing, I pleaded for her to deliver a verdict.

'You ask too much of me,' she murmured. 'I can offer you sympathy. I can pity you. But I cannot judge you. I was not part of that. You lived in a world and time incomprehensible to me. What you did was to try and survive in those conditions. And I don't know how the world, now, would view that.'

'I did nothing to prevent those conditions.'

'Had you tried, you would have been treated as a saboteur and traitor.'

'Or I could simply have left my job and gone away to fight the war as a soldier.'

'You were the youngest station master in Germany. You took pride in your work.'

'I did once, yes.'

'Your trouble was, when it was no longer possible to derive that satisfaction, it was already too late.'

'I was committed. Locked into the system. The excuse we all gave to absolve ourselves from blame.'

She was silent for a moment. Then she asked, 'When exactly did you find out where the trains were going and what was happening to the people inside them?'

The one question I dared not ask myself. 'I don't know. I honestly don't know if I ever really knew. There were things we couldn't allow ourselves to know. We heard rumours, yes. Monstrous rumours. But it was happening somewhere else. Not where I was. My station was just a transit point on the way to the concentration camps. And we didn't know what was happening in those camps.'

'The guards who took Rachel away. They knew where she was going. They were laughing.'

I put my hand up to cover my face. 'Oh God, I don't know if they knew. I couldn't permit myself to think there was no hope for her. There had to be. It was just a camp.'

'When they took her from you, you carved a swastika on your breast.'

I tore open my shirt, as I had then. 'There it is. Look for yourself.'

She fingered the weal under my chest hair. There wasn't much of it left. Just a shapeless ridge of tissue. It could have been anything.

She lowered her lips and kissed my brow. 'I believe you.'

'Believe what? That I am guilty? Innocent? What?'

'That you have suffered. That you have lived with the guilt of it eating into you. That you have paid over and over for what you did. That you can no longer go on punishing yourself.'

'Guilty then?'

She threw up her hand in exasperation. 'Yes, guilty. What else would you have me say?'

I pulled her hand down to my mouth. 'Thank you. Thank you.'

'But with extenuating circumstances.'

'Please don't extenuate. Don't exonerate.'

It was getting late into the afternoon.

We had brought no food with us.

She hadn't expected us to stay this long.

'Come on,' she said. 'Eduardo will be looking for you.'

'But the butterflies?'

'I'll come back for them another day. I'll leave the set-up as it is. Simply hitch the ropes around the tree so that all we have to do is pull ourselves up again. It will be easier for you next time.'

'I hope so.'

'Do you suppose the Indians will find the ropes and cut them down?'

'They may think they're spirit ropes and run for their lives.'

She laughed.

She was right. The descent was much, much easier.

But in that short space of time my life had changed!

The tree had lifted me in its arms and held me up to the sun.

ADAGIO

I

She followed me back to the house, accepting my invitation to supper.

Eduardo ran to meet me at the door but stopped when he saw her, surprised that she should be arriving so late.

Stooping to hold him by the shoulders, she said, 'Uncle Kristian had an adventure today. He climbed a tree. A very high tree.'

He looked at me with hurt in his eyes. I had lied to him. I told him I was going to O Varayo on business.

I bent to join her. 'I couldn't take you, Eduardo, because it was dangerous. I didn't think I could do it myself.'

He tried to slip from her hold. He wanted to run back to the kitchen to hide his disappointment.

'Tomorrow you can come with us if you like,' she said. 'We're going back to the tree and we can take you along. Would you like that?'

He looked from her to me, not knowing if he could trust us.

I whispered to her, 'Is it safe?'

She nodded. 'We'll make sure it is. I'll keep a harness on him while we're up there. It will be your chance, Eduardo, to show your Uncle Kristian that you are braver than he is. He yelled out in fright. Didn't you, Kristian?'

I found and squeezed her hand.

Eduardo needed more information. 'Is it big?' he asked. 'Like the tree that stands alone?'

'Bigger. The biggest tree in the world. From there you can see the whole forest.'

He smiled and nodded. 'I will come.'

At supper, brought to us by a beaming Estancia, who seemed overjoyed to have Ruth in the house, I said, 'You're quite a woman. I've never met one like you.'

'You haven't met many women. You haven't kept in touch with what's happening out there. We're claiming at last what has been denied us for centuries. Why don't you come back with me?'

I shook my head. 'Not unless you've been deceiving me all this time, tricking that confession out of me by letting me dangle there.'

She considered for a moment and then said, 'What made you choose me for your Nemesis?'

I shrugged. 'You're Jewish. You know how to handle a pistol. You look as if you've been trained as a commando.'

'You have to be to survive in New York. But why me? There must have been at least some others who have been strangers to this backwater, who could equally have come for the purpose you imagined.'

'None like you. None who had come looking for anything as improbable as butterflies. The few visitors we see are here strictly on business. What else would bring them?'

'*You* chose to come here.'

'Precisely for that reason.'

'But that was more than forty years ago.'

I nodded. 'Time is running out. The river is running dry. You *had* to be the one I was expecting. I had waited so long.'

2

I took her up to the music room, but it was impossible to show her, by candlelight, why I called it that. The shadows cast by the leaves seemed gothic, more like some harrowing piece of Schoenberg than Ravel or Debussy.

'I don't go much for music,' she said, 'but if you hear it in your head I can see why this room would be the place to listen. Not by night though.'

I agreed. Not by night.

I had left the journal lying on the escritoire. She picked it up. 'Mind if I look?' she asked.

I could have stopped her, but I didn't.

She started at the beginning, turning over the pages so slowly I was surprised to be reminded how much I had put into them.

No doubt curious to see what we were up to, Estancia brought us mugs of coffee. I lack the apparatus for entertaining with any gentility. Ordinarily the only visitor who comes is Father Lorenzo.

I suggested to Estancia that she fetch the folding canvas chairs for us to sit on, but Ruth heard me and indicated, with a shake of her hand, that she wasn't to bother. She emphasised the point by sliding down the wall, against which she had been leaning, until she adopted a yoga posture on the bare floorboards. She never took her eyes from the book.

Estancia looked to me for guidance. I put my finger to my lips and waved her away.

She left the spare candle she had brought with her, stooping to place it on the floor beside me. I watched how it altered the patterns of shadow, turning the grotesqueries of Schoenberg into something less discordant. And when the flame settled, and the leaves added their almost imperceptible variations of movement in the slightest breath of a night breeze, I saw in them the textures of the Adagio from Beethoven's 'Hammerklavier' Sonata, the calm that follows the stress.

It was strange having her with me, sharing that private space without hearing what I could hear. She never looked at me once, reading on, page after page. At times closing her eyes and leaning her head back against the wall for an interval before continuing. At times, when she reached the later pages, smiling at my account of her. I could almost follow the lines with her. They seemed at one with the music in my head.

At last she closed the covers and bent forward over the book, clutching it to her breast. She held out her hand towards me and I reached to take it, letting our fingers entwine like the interlocking branches of the tree.

'It's getting late,' I said.

She nodded, her hair falling forward like a shawl across her face.

'Will you stay here tonight?'

She lifted her head, tossing the hair from her eyes to look at me. Her cheeks were glistening. She released her hand from my fingers to brush them. 'Yes.'

'I don't have a proper guest room.'

She looked beyond the tree to the doomed bed, poised above the abyss into which it must soon sink. Smiling slowly, as if with an effort, she said, 'I can see why.'

Before replacing the journal, she asked me why I had chosen to write it in English.

Because it was necessary, I said, to adhere to my new persona, my Swiss/English pretensions.

Even with something as intensely personal as this journal?

I nodded. Looking at it through another language had helped me detach myself.

3

Once Esquamillo had silenced the generator, she wanted me to leave the candle burning by the bedside. My bedroom, she said, was as big as a dance hall. Big enough for bats to blunder in through the open windows. She wasn't afraid of bats. She just didn't want them landing on her.

Climbing in beside her, I joked about being cast in the role of an ancient vampire.

She touched the scar above my nipple. 'Still marked by the stake which failed to kill you.'

'I'm a survivor. Old enough to be your grandfather.'

Nestling her cheek on my chest, she said, 'I never knew what it was like to have a grandfather. Both of mine died when I was very young. Leaving me with something missing from my life.'

'Grandfathers don't usually sleep with their granddaughters.' She hugged me. 'So we have that advantage, don't we?'

She had cradled me in the tree. I now returned the gesture, clasping her to me, feeling, wondrously, the stirrings of sensations I had not experienced in years.

'Did Imelda die in the music room?' she asked.

'No, in this bed. The music room was like that when we arrived. I left it that way. I wanted its umbilical cord with nature. It was my emergency exit. A part of the forest that had intruded into my life and was waiting patiently to carry me away. As a last resort I would surrender myself to it and never look back.'

'I could see that from your journal. Did she join you there? Did she hear what you heard?'

'She was like you. She had no real taste for music. But it pleased her that I had. That at least I had that to fall back on. If my playing became too agitated, and there was nothing she could do to relieve my mood, she would retire to her altar or the back of the house. Estancia was just a young serving girl then, and not much help to Imelda in trying to cope with me, but at least she was a shoulder to cry on.'

'It must have been difficult for your wife to give up everything and follow you here. Yet of all the things recorded in your journal, your account of her is the briefest. I sense also that it was the hardest to write.'

'It was. I loved her. But I never understood her. Nor she me. And when she died, so young, bearing the child that could have saved us both, I felt I had murdered both of them by allowing her to love me, by letting myself love in return. As if just by mentioning her name I had made her the object of the vengeance that pursues me wherever I go.'

She propped herself on her chin to look into my eyes. 'In that case,' she said, 'we had better make a pact. Not to love each other. Or at least not to let each other know it if we do.'

Pulling her head down, I kissed her nose. 'I promise I will never even mention the thought that is in my mind at this very moment.'

I wanted to use all my long-neglected skills on her. Skills I had practised on my wife to reward her for her fidelity, providing some measure of compensation for the loneliness of her isolation in that fastness of forest. Where Imelda had sought love, I gave her ecstasy, assuring her our very names dictated the pitch and tempo of our emotions, pretending we were lovers in a Wagnerian opera. Kristian and Imelda.

I wanted to bring those same talents to bear on Ruth, but she stopped me. She took control of our love-making, keeping it *piano* rather than *sforzando*, indicating, gently but unmistakably, that she looked for affection more than passion.

Taking my lead from her, I felt myself caught up in a slow, swirling current that bore us through the night, half sleeping, half waking, but always in each other's arms.

In the early hours of the morning she nudged me. 'You were whispering in your sleep.'

'What was I saying?'

'I don't know. I think it was in German.'

I tried to remember my dream. 'We were saying goodbye. I was holding you, pleading with you not to leave.'

'Where were we?'

'On a station platform.'

She gently nibbled my chin with her lips, murmuring, 'Kristian, Kristian. You left that station behind you long ago. Don't keep going back. If you won't come to America with me at least stay here in your music room. Where I can find you again. I can't find you there. You don't belong there. You never did.'

Which was what Imelda had tried to tell me, dying without finding the words to express it. Or even knowing what had led to it.

'Why,' I queried, 'did you allow me to attach myself to you without ever asking questions?'

'I sensed you were hiding something. That you had reason to. I had no reason to pry. Your mistake was in believing that I had.'

'I couldn't understand your complete lack of curiosity. It was as if you knew everything about me, and had no need to ask. It confirmed my belief that you had come not for the butterflies but for me.'

'For one old bat living alone in his secret cave?' She laughed. 'Oh, I'm sorry, my dear, I didn't mean it that way. But you do tend to have a rather distorted view of your own importance. You have to accept the fact that you were a relatively minor functionary. The civilised world has not been sending out search parties to look for you. The Jewish nation is not crying for your blood.'

'You don't know what it was like for me, reading of the others who were tracked down, one by one. Knowing my time must come. Wishing that it would.'

'But the prisoners who shuffled past you had no idea who you were, and would now be quite unable to identify you if they remembered at all. They had other, real monsters to contend with.'

I prised her arm from around my neck and sat up, feeling suddenly impotent and used. 'That's not what I meant.'

She raised herself beside me and kissed my shoulder. 'Kristian, I'm sorry. If that sounded callous and insensitive it was only meant to be kind. I want to relieve you of this burden you have taken upon yourself. You can't carry on these shoulders all the sins of the Third Reich. No one expects you to.'

I found it difficult to bring the words out. 'How can I explain to you that it was I who accused *myself*! That I *needed* to, because I could not turn my back on what I had done, even if I was the only one left who still remembered!'

She weighed my words. 'I see. You *needed* me to be your Nemesis? You weren't looking for forgiveness?'

'I wanted forgiveness, yes, but also release.'

'You ask too much. I cannot give you that. You make it sound as if you wanted me to be your executioner. That's terrible, Kristian! Terrible! Father Lorenzo is right to be worried about you. You are too much in love with death.'

'He's been talking to you?'

'Naturally. Everyone in O Varayo has been talking to me. It's a very small place.'

'About me?'

'Oh, come on, Kristian, your ego is impossible. Father Lorenzo has been talking about you, yes. I sometimes think you're the only reason he stays here.'

'Not me. The Indians.'

'The Indians *and* you. You're the real prize he's after. He has learned almost nothing about you and is consumed with hunger for your salvation. You never needed me. All you needed was Father Lorenzo, and he has been here all the time.'

'He is a man of God. He would crumple under the weight of my confession. It would destroy him.'

'You underestimate his strength. Try him.'

'Father Lorenzo would be shocked just to see us at this moment.'

She giggled. 'Perhaps you're right.'

'He told me I was an old goat, throwing myself at you.'

'And so you were.'

'Then why did you allow it?'

'I needed your protection. Otherwise I would have spent all my time fending off those lechers who crowd around the Trocadero. Haven't they ever seen a woman before?'

'Not one like you. I swear it.'

There came a hesitant knocking at the door.

'Eduardo,' I whispered. 'I told him to be up early, and ready to leave by four.'

She held a finger to her lips. 'Pass me your dressing gown so I can slip into the bathroom. And then let him in.'

'We haven't slept!'

'Wait till we get there. The tree can rock you to sleep while Eduardo and I watch out for butterflies.'

LEGATO

I

It has taken time to conquer the fear of it, especially in watching Eduardo, but now I am exhilarated by the life we lead.

And I understand why the English say that one cannot see the wood for the trees. For this is the first time I have really seen the forest.

Our days up there have been the happiest since my childhood.

Or is it only that I am old, and beginning to forget?

My memories curl up and detach themselves one by one, falling away like dead leaves. And I do not miss them.

I wish only for the continuation, for ever, of this part of me that is still left. And the knowledge that it cannot last – indeed will soon end – serves merely to intensify the experience.

We have moved base four times already, with Ruth making the initial ascent to see if the crown offers sufficient interest and will support the three of us. For she accepts that we are 'all in this together' as she puts it.

Each day we depart before sunrise and return with the dusk. Estancia packs our lunch and reminds Eduardo to be careful.

He is fast becoming the most agile of our trio, with a natural instinct for climbing that hardly requires teaching, although Ruth ensures he stays in the harness at all times.

I am not so sure this is wise because it encourages him to take risks he would not otherwise dare. Once, on the ascent, he started walking out along a branch, performing a balancing act and calling out, 'Look, Uncle Kristian. Look at me.' Ruth threatened to reel him in if he didn't come back of his own accord.

It is a patient wait up there. Not, she says, as productive as the Genting forest reserve in Malaysia. The butterflies are fewer, and seldom come close enough for her camera. But she tracks and identifies them with her binoculars and declares herself satisfied with the results she is getting.

The day will come I know when, with the descending sun, she will look at her watch and say, 'Time to go!' And mean much more than the journey on foot back to the house. But until then we are ourselves arboreal creatures, living in the sunlight and huddling together under our plastic sheets (Ruth's rucksack is a cornucopia of useful supplies) during the brief but often violent cloudbursts.

Eduardo loves the thunderstorms, but up there among the leaves I have developed, for the first time, a greater respect for them. Two weeks ago a lightning bolt struck an adjoining *ceiba* tree, only slightly taller than ours, and stripped it instantly in a great explosion of incinerated foliage. Eduardo did not see. He had his head buried in my shoulder, chuckling with delight.

He likes best the tsunami that precedes the rain, the sudden squall that whips the rigging of our green masthead and threatens to dislodge us from the crow's-nest. The dipping and plunging exhilarate him, and he cries out at the sight of plucked vegetation driven like flocks of birds on the wind.

Mostly, however, we rock with the gentle motion of a barque, tethered on currents that ripple through the forest like probing offshoots of an invisible river, restlessly seeking new courses.

Up there one can be deceived into believing that this is still the New World, as seen and documented by Humboldt, Darwin and those who followed them. The forest seems to roll on for ever, untroubled by the loggers, the prospectors and the waves of settlers who are descending like locusts on the land.

And it is inhabited by more species of animal and insect than I had ever imagined. How many others have already disappeared we cannot know, for Ruth says some have now remained so long unseen that their survival is in question.

While butterflies are her chief concern, she encourages me to keep my own spotter's log, so I will learn more of my surroundings. It is disgraceful, she claims, that I have discovered so little of the riches within my 'own back yard'.

Eduardo, she adds, would learn more from his tribe in a week than he has learned from me in a year. And alas I cannot deny it.

To avenge myself for this I take pride in reminding her that already in my notebook I have recorded more moths than she has logged butterflies. She helps me identify them, even points them out to me when their astonishing camouflage makes them seem one with the bark on which they spread their mottled wings.

Of all she has seen so far, the butterfly that most enthralls her is the blue morpho, whose iridescent sapphire enchanted Darwin and still looks the brightest jewel in the jungle.

Not quite as beautiful, but more interesting in their relationship with the flora of the upper galleries, are the heliconid butterflies. Highly coloured, either with streaks of black and yellow or splashed with red, these have perfected a technique of dining off poisonous passion-flower vines.

Capturing a caterpillar of the species, Ruth explained that its vivid hues result from the toxins it digests from the vine leaves. Infusing both the caterpillar and the butterfly into which it develops, the poison makes them indigestible to their own predators.

She has also pointed out to me the extraordinary Hercules caterpillar, one glimpse of whose porcelain blue body, spiked with vicious yellow horns, would be enough to repel any would-be assailant. From this astonishing larva emerges the largest moth in the world.

She never keeps these specimens, however rare, and is always scrupulously careful to replace them exactly as she found them. Nothing could be further removed from my preconception of the naturalist as collector and trophy hunter.

Also recorded in my notebook are a variety of other creatures, ranging from the red and green arrow poison frog and *tachimenys* tree snake to the crested flycatcher and harpy eagle. For me the most disquieting find was the decaying corpse of a three-toed sloth, its claws still clamped like a vice to the branch on which it had died.

Once a troop of howler monkeys discovered our presence and unleashed a display of vocal braggadocio that made Eduardo put his fingers to his ears. They seemed deeply, and understandably, disturbed to find that the deadliest of bipedal carnivores have finally invaded their stronghold so far above terra firma where we belong.

However remarkable the extent of its adaptation and specialisation, the fauna is outclassed by the flora. When it comes to spectacle, nothing can surpass the awesome beauty of a hanging garden of epiphytic orchids.

Tiny, jewel-like in the intensity of their colouring, these cluster together with the uncanny brilliance of anemones crowding an inverted sea bed. Probing shafts of sunlight, for which they fiercely compete, turn them into incandescent tapestries woven between the contrasts of light and shade.

Ingenious opportunists of the plant world, they batten on to any vegetation that will afford a foothold. Ruth tells me that dozens of species have been counted on one tree, jostling for the favoured upper branches nearest the sun.

More remarkable is the extent to which they have refined their mechanisms for achieving pollination. Unwitting insects are enticed inside them, through beguiling combinations of colour and scent, and briefly imprisoned – sometimes half drowned in tiny reservoirs of secreted fluids – before being released with their burdens of pollen firmly attached.

The stunning diversity and profusion of life in this lost world opening up to me has made a deep impression. I feel privileged to enter a sanctuary from which man has been exiled by the very attainment he regards as his evolutionary triumph. The bipedal skill that drove him down to a pedestrian existence on the forest floor.

Was this what God intended?

What if the Garden of Eden was not a geographical location but an altitude? Lucifer too once belonged in the heights before his banishment to the lower darkness.

Did we fall – literally fall – from grace?

The possibility struck me with such painful force that Ruth saw it in my face, and asked me what was wrong.

When I told her, tried to explain it to her, she hugged me without speaking.

If I need proof of the characteristic that distinguishes us, that aroused the opposition of the howler monkeys who discovered our presence, I have only to observe Eduardo. It seems in his blood to devise ways of bringing down the creatures he sees. Too young to fashion spears, he aims twigs at them, which he hurls in an imitation of spear-throwing.

When I wag my finger to discourage him, pointing out that we forest creatures must live together, Ruth tells me not to interfere with his native instinct.

'He is destined to be a hunter,' she said. 'And he will kill only what he has to. It is not the Indians who are destroying the life of this forest. It's the big land barons with their widescale plundering of whole regions which they will never visit from their distant offices in São Paulo or Rio de Janeiro.'

Perhaps she is right. Eduardo is, after all, destined to grow up in this jungle and be part of it for so long as it lasts. And he must survive in it with his Indian wit. Also, perhaps, with some vestige of the skills we have taught him, that will help him hold his own against those who try to wrest from him his natural inheritance.

Yet when I look at his face, and trace where the softness of childhood will yield to the contours of youth, I see too where the war-paint might lie across his cheeks and how the feathers would look on his brow. And it saddens me how quickly the jungle is reclaiming its own.

Will Esquamillo use the money I leave to send him downriver to the college in Manáus? Will he keep the boy on the land to till the soil and follow in his footsteps? Or will his mother resist his surrender to that limbo the Indian must always occupy on the edge of civilisation and, instead, send him back into the forest to learn the ways of her tribe?

Whatever it is, I will not be here to see. I must let nature take its course. I am like the sterile salmon that has scaled the last cataracts to the shallows from which the threads of the river are drawn. And as I wait to die I must watch the spawn of others released into the stream to populate the distant sea. Drawing comfort only from the knowledge that the cycle will go on without me.

2

Three days ago, when we were busy establishing our base in the second of two *ceiba* trees Ruth has chosen for our research, Eduardo drew our attention to a distant point of light, flashing intermittently like a signal lamp at sea. Focusing her field glasses, Ruth confessed she didn't know what to make of it, except that what appeared to be the tip of some artificial structure was showing above the treetops. Was there a radio transmitter in this locality?

I dismissed the suggestion. It would have been impossible for even the most secret of installations to be erected here without my knowledge. And why would anyone wish to do so in this unlikely backwater? I proposed instead that it was a piece of wreckage from a downed aircraft that had escaped the eye of the search teams.

Mine was the correct assumption, but it took some diligent searching before, just this morning, we identified the location with sufficient precision to reach the wreck. Confirmation came in the form of a wheel, and part of an undercarriage, draped over a branch about ten metres above the forest floor.

If the Indians have ever seen it they must have given it a wide berth as something that does not belong in their environment and therefore does not call either for investigation or a report to those interfering authorities whose unwelcome attentions they can do without.

For it has been there many, many years. On the evidence, just before, during or immediately following the war.

It was, of course, Ruth who reached the wreck first, after exploring a false trail up the tree where the wheel was lodged, only to discover, when she reached the top, that its source was some four trees away. The angle of descent must have hurled the undercarriage that extra distance.

She pulled us up after her, cautioning us to watch out for the scattered remnants of broken wing and fuselage we encountered on the way.

I had the curious sensation of a dive executed in reverse; of participating in a salvage hunt that took us to the surface rather than the depths of our chosen ocean.

I was ready for anything. Air liners have gone missing in these jungles without leaving a visible trace. But the wreck, when I reached it, was almost disappointingly small, reminding me of a crushed telephone booth. A resemblance accentuated by the skeletal remains of its occupant, who hung forward through the shattered windscreen as though despairing of ever achieving his connection.

The rain, the sun and the scavengers had leeched his aerial coffin almost entirely clear of any evidence of who he was or what he was doing here, and the parasitic plants and creepers had smothered the remains in a patina as thick and as obstinate as the crust of barnacles that closes over the trophies of the sea bed. What had caught Eduardo's eye, through some freak of light across that intervening forest, was a shattered remnant of broken glass, like the last desperate message delivered to a remote beach, bearing an SOS from the long-deceased survivor of a shipwreck.

As its rightful discoverer, the boy was aggrieved to be denied access to the wreck itself, but Ruth rightly decided that the precariously lodged cockpit was no place for him. So he was left lashed to a fork of the tree a few metres below, where we could keep an eye on him and deliver an edited account of our findings.

There was one important clue. What I can only describe as the equivalent of a ship's log, in Portuguese, except that this was more in the form of a pocket diary. I found it wedged in a receptacle above the dashboard, which in itself was a clue to the antiquity of the aircraft, even before we noticed the shattered struts that identified it as a biplane.

The diary did not yield its secrets easily. Only when we got back to the house this afternoon was I able to prise apart the thick, mouldering wad of pages and decipher the script. And so far all I have been able to distinguish with any accuracy is the last entry, which, sadly, is left undated. The sense of it is as follows:

> Today's flight confirmed my suspicions. I returned to the co-ordinates I recorded earlier, but in better weather conditions. There is definitely a man-made structure down there. Traces of stone foundations in typical grid outline. Could the Incas have come so far east? If so it must date from just before the Conquest. Possibly *Huayna Capac*. I spent so much time circling, and trying to take photographs, that I ran dangerously low on fuel. Must ensure full tanks for tomorrow's flight.

When I extracted the last sentence of this barely legible text I looked up to see Ruth in tears, just as she was when she had finished reading my journal. Perhaps it reminded her of the notebook they found on her uncle, after his body had been picked clean by the condors.

She insisted we report the find immediately, but I patiently dissuaded her. Whatever he found is now, in all probability, lost again. Even if the diary surrenders the precise co-ordinates the chances are the site will either be inaccessible, entirely obliterated by vegetation or already visited by subsequent explorers. It might also be a hundred or more kilometres from here. Perhaps the plane had crashed because, despite his best intentions, he finally ran out of fuel on the return trip. In which case the ruins he discovered might be, as is more likely, in the foothills of the Andes.

From the evidence of the aircraft itself, and the extent of the decay, it has been there at least forty years. Probably more. Why rush it? Why call down upon our heads all the appalling spotlight of a seven-day media circus which will, in all probability, destroy rather than salvage the fragile traces that will help unravel the mystery?

She remained unconvinced, suspecting that my motives were personal and selfish. Why, when I was ready to embrace her as my deliverer, am I now so wary of delivering this unknown aviator from his limbo in the treetops? She is less concerned with what he stumbled across than with the identity of the man himself.

For all I know there are surviving parents, a wife and family, still waiting for news, still racked by the ordeal of not knowing what became of him. And what has my history to do with his? How could the two possibly conflict?

I asked for time. Time at least to painstakingly resurrect the record of the diary. Just separating the bonded pages will call for all the patient skills I acquired when I salvaged the library I found in this house.

The camera! She suddenly remembered his reference to photographs. Could that also have survived? Is it conceivable that his last film is still in there, still unspoilt? The chances, I reminded her, are so remote as to be discounted. Even if it survived the crash and was recoverable, the casing would have rusted through years ago.

She has allowed me another month to work on the diary, and has made it clear she will expect daily reports on my progress.

In return I have extracted from her a promise to say nothing about our discovery, either at the Trocadero or elsewhere in O Varayo.

What about Eduardo? she asks. How can we be sure that even now he has not given as full an account as he can render to his parents?

Because, I explain, when we descended from the tree, and she was busy packing the gear, I took him aside and convinced him this was to be our secret. At least until we knew enough to safely confide it to others.

Do I trust him that much?

Of course, I reply. When two people have shared the secrets of this music room there can be no chance of betrayal.

But even as I said it I knew what a lie that was.

How many times have I betrayed him already? And how many more before we part?

LES ADIEUX

I

When we descended last night, from our third *ceiba* tree, festooned with Spanish moss, orchids and parasitic vines, she told me she would be returning to the Trocadero instead of to the house. Her notes needed proper sorting and she was running low on film.

I sensed that the reasons she gave disguised what she could not bring herself to convey, but I said nothing, hoping that I was wrong, that she merely needed time to think where we were going next.

This morning, when Eduardo came to the room and found me alone, I lit the candle that we normally left burning and lifted him on to the bed with me.

I explained that we would not be climbing today. Instead, we would be going to town to surprise Ruth at the hotel.

Lying awake in the pre-dawn darkness, I had been gripped by the fear that she may already have left, slipping down the river in the night without a word.

Reason told me she would never leave like that. It was not in her nature to do so. Besides, what about the diary I was still busy translating? I still had a week to run before the deadline she has allowed for reporting our findings.

Instinct told me otherwise. That I am not the only one practised in the gentle arts of deceit.

We hurried down the canal, scattering the frogs, disturbing the mists that layered its banks. Eduardo ran to keep up with me until, exhausted, he became a weight upon my arm. Impatiently I hoisted him upon my shoulders and pressed on, surprising the passing tappers with my urgency.

The hotel door was locked, like the portal to a deserted keep. Eduardo became alarmed by my shouting and frantic rattling of the handle.

Eventually Remedios came, wide-eyed at the commotion I was causing.

'Is she here?' I asked.

He shrugged. But of course. Why the panic?

He showed me into the lobby and switched on the lights, to reveal her standing at the top of the stairs, already dressed.

I could think of nothing to say that would excuse my presence there.

'Come upstairs,' she said, turning back towards her room.

Following her, I found an open suitcase on her bed, surrounded by piles of clothing and the waterproof pouches in which she stored her film.

I didn't need to put the question.

She looked at me, as if to ask why I had brought the child.

I put my answer into words. 'Blackmail,' I said. 'I was hoping to make you change your mind.'

She got up and walked past me to the stairwell, addressing Remedios, who was still standing there, confused as to what was happening.

'I'm sorry to be a nuisance,' she said. 'But do you suppose we could have breakfast? For three?'

He was silent for a moment and then nodded. 'Half an hour. I will get the stove going.'

She came back into the room. 'There was no need for this. I was coming back to the house to tell you.'

'With everything packed? At this hour of the morning?'

She looked back accusingly. 'Have I ever lied to you?'

'I have lied. Many times. I know how easy it is.'

She looked down at the boy. 'Eduardo, why don't you help Senhór Remedios in the kitchen? You must be hungry and I am sure he has some nice warm buns for you.'

Eduardo looked from her to me.

'That's a good idea, Eduardo,' I said. 'You know where it is.'

He went, knowing we wanted him out of the way.

'I left it to the last moment,' she said, 'because I am not very good at partings.'

'I'm not asking you to defend your reasons. Why should I have a monopoly on betrayal?'

The anger flashed in her eyes. 'That's not fair. Don't judge me by your standards.' And then, reflecting on what she had said, 'No. That's not what I meant. Oh God, why are you doing this to me? You're not giving me a chance. I was coming to tell you. I swear it.'

She sank down on the bed and I sat beside her, touching her shoulder. 'You're right. It's not fair of me. I panicked. I was afraid you might already have left.'

'I've got enough from this trip. I exhausted the potential weeks ago. If it hadn't been for you I would have been long gone. There is nothing in the canopy that I haven't already seen. I was letting myself drift. Spinning out time because I didn't want it to end. I can't afford that. I have work to do, a report to write, a career to pursue. The woods are lovely, dark and deep, but I have promises to keep.'

'And I, of course, have not so far to go before I sleep.'

She touched my hand. 'Very far, Kristian. You're very fit for your age. Amazing really. Like a man half your years.'

'That's only because I have lived half a life.'

She looked into my eyes. 'Yes, I won't argue with that. You have buried yourself here. Forcing your tired ghosts to dance for you when they wished only to sleep. I hope I have made you see that?'

I nodded. 'You have made me see more than that. You have awakened me to appetites I thought I had lost.'

Squeezing my fingers, she said, 'Yes, that too. I thought I had found a grandfather and instead I found a lover.'

'What about our discovery?' I asked. 'How can you leave now, just as we are about to unveil it to the world?'

'You have no intention of unveiling it. You have been playing for time, barely squeezing out a sentence of translation each day.'

'Yes I have. I freely admit it. I have been selfish. Unreasonable. Denying the world an archaeological find of the greatest significance and the family of that unfortunate man the outcome of his fate. But I am ready to make amends, I swear it. I am ready to tell the world today, if only it would keep you here. You cannot go and leave me to face that on my own. It is really your find more than mine. Yours and Eduardo's. It could set you on a whole new career.'

'And what will it do for Eduardo?'

'Give him a platform from which to speak for the Indians. Renew public interest in what their lost civilisations achieved, long before the white man ever came here.'

'You really believe that?'

'I'd like to, but perhaps not. Not now anyway. When he's older maybe. Old enough to become their champion.'

'In that case there's no rush, is there? I can come back. When you're ready. When you feel you want me enough to take on the cameras and the reporters. After all, they're not going to be interested in us so much as they are in the man who has been missing for the best part of half a century. And of course the ruins he reported in his diary.'

I looked into her eyes, wanting desperately to believe her. 'You'll come back?'

She nodded. 'When you're ready. When I've wrapped up my own project. There's no particular hurry, is there?'

She seemed to allow for the possibility that I would contradict this. As if there were reason for urgency.

'No particular hurry,' I affirmed. 'Why should there be?'

'In that case let's have breakfast.'

2

After breakfast we walked with Eduardo, following the track along the dried up watercourse as far as the point where the river has carved a new channel for itself. It has been a long time since the boy last saw the river. He stared mesmerised at the great swirling discs of brown current, spinning shattered tree trunks and rafts of uprooted vegetation in its cogs and gears.

It was an ugly river, swollen by cloudbursts in the distant foothills, draining the life from the green heart of this continent. Eduardo threw stones at it, as if to drive it away.

Gazing at the current, not looking at me, Ruth said, 'The man in the saloon, the murderer of the girl found on your estate. You have done nothing to trace him, have you?'

She had read the pages of my journal. How could I deny it?

'You don't want him traced, do you?'

I shrugged. 'It's a big country, as you see for yourself.'

'He came looking for you. He offered himself to you.'

'To prove my incompetence. The man doesn't have any respect for human life. Including his own.'

'So why don't you stop him, before he kills again?'

I hadn't thought of that.

'Next time,' she said, 'it could be Eduardo. He could snap his neck like a twig. He could have snapped mine.'

I remained silent. Suddenly I saw, in my inertia combined with fatalism, how foolish I had been to risk the lives of others.

'When I get to Manáus, I'm going to report him to the authorities. I don't care about the wrecked plane. Lives don't depend on its discovery. Whoever may be left behind by that death is long reconciled to the pilot's fate. But the girl who died on your estate left a far more urgent inheritance. I care about her, and I care for what might happen to others like her. I can give a pretty fair description of her killer, even from those few seconds before he came behind me.'

'Yes, do that,' I said, all my resolution draining away with that river, whose full, ravenous power suddenly tore into me, eroding the last of my free will.

'And deny you the luxury of playing sacrificial lamb in his place?'

There was no cruelty intended in the way she phrased the question, but it struck right to the heart of my hypocrisy.

'You're right. I wasn't thinking straight. He must be stopped.'

She took my hand and turned to face me. 'I spoke to you this morning of the promises I have yet to keep. I now ask one of you.'

'What is it?'

'If he *does* come back, if there *is* to be a confrontation, I want you to kill him. Don't let him shoot first. You owe it to the Indians, to that girl whose throat he cut without compunction. You owe it to Eduardo and to those others he might yet destroy. Don't allow him to play the executioner you have been seeking for your own sins. Those are over. You have atoned for them. But this man is capable of killing again. And not just you.'

'You forget that this is not the Wild West.'

'No, it's much wilder. There is no sheriff in O Varayo. You have to take on that responsibility. The Indians don't want you. All that nonsense about the birth of the thirteenth moon. What does that mean to them? They want the man who killed their child. They looked to you because they had no one else to turn to, and you have let them down. Because you were too much in love with the possibility of contriving your own death.'

I didn't know what to say. I began to tremble with the impact of her words.

She pulled me to her and hugged me. 'Oh my dear, I am sorry. But I fear for you, for the way you have blinded yourself to everything but your past. You said it yourself in your journal. The evil is still there. The world is rotten with it, and getting worse. Why do you think I carry a pistol? Only for the pumas and the jaguars I may meet in this jungle? No, more for the danger I may face in that other jungle of New York. The man who sought you out in the saloon would be at home in the streets of Manhattan or the Bronx. I have seen that look on faces in the subway, even in elevators where I am glad not to be alone with them.'

When we returned to the hotel, she said, 'I have to finish packing.'

'Yes I know. I will go. As you say, why prolong the agony?'

'I will write.'

'Please do that.'

'And I will return. When you're ready to reveal our discovery.'

I nodded. But in my heart I knew it was not to be. Not, at any rate, while I am still alive.

I have failed her. I have failed them all. A catalogue of failure.

She dropped on her heels to kiss Eduardo. 'I have to go away for a while, Eduardo. I will come back to you some day. By then perhaps you will be a big boy.'

He tried to take this in. No one until now has ever left him. He doesn't know what the word means.

In the darkened lobby of the hotel, deserted at that time of the morning, we embraced. She pressed her pistol into my hand. 'Take it,' she said. 'I can easily replace it.'

'Why?'

'To use if he returns. At least to defend yourself. But with the *intention* to kill him. Don't let your life go to waste. Use the chance to redeem yourself.'

'Esquamillo has a shotgun. I can borrow that.'

'Use both. Use everything you can to destroy him. Have no pity in your heart. This man *enjoys* killing.'

I looked into her eyes and saw that there, at least, I would be redeemed if only I could keep this one promise. I nodded. 'I promise.'

I held her, kissed her and released her, turning quickly so that I would not have to look back.

On the long journey home Eduardo spoke only once. 'Will we go climbing tomorrow? Will we see the aeroplane?'

But I could not reply.

When Estancia had put the child to bed I summoned Esquamillo and asked him to fetch the tapper who had come to me in the saloon to inform me of the killer's presence.

He came, the insincerity of his smile confirming a suspicion, which had lurked in my mind ever since, that he was in league with the killer.

I had reason to believe, I said, that he knew the man's whereabouts.

He shrugged. It might be possible to track him down, yes, if I really wished it.

I was about to offer him money, but then I thought, no, it's not the money. He's testing me, to see if I have the courage.

Yes, I said, I really wished it.

And still the suspicion lingers in my mind.

The pistol.

Intended for him, or for me?

That she has waited right to the last, when it was clear I was too cowardly to pay for my sins any other way, suggests the latter.

Why do I allow this nagging doubt to chafe the painful memory of our parting? So as to harden myself to the prospect of renewing my life without her?

PIANISSIMO

I

The tapper returned to me two nights ago, conveying a message from the killer. He is willing to meet me at dawn tomorrow, in the clearing with the solitary mahogany tree.

My heart leapt at the fitness of the setting. It was as if he had read my mind. But then I realised it was the only place off the estate where we would be undisturbed and still have a clear line of fire.

I was to come alone. Or, at most, I could bring the boy with me.

As if I would expose the one life I most wish to protect!

Why, I asked, is he so willing to keep this rendezvous? What am I to this man that he should so gladly seek me out?

The *seringueiro* shrugged. The man has told him only that he has a debt to settle with me. Many years ago his father encroached on to Indian lands bordering my estate, and I pronounced in favour of the Indians. As a result the family were dispossessed of their squatters' rights and forced to return to Manáus.

When the father died in poverty, the son vowed he would avenge himself on me. He would find occasion to pick a quarrel, forcing me to seek him out.

The Indian girl, I asked. Had she been killed just because of this grievance against me?

The messenger nodded, the smirk never leaving his face. She came from the tribe to whom I had returned the land.

In my anger I could understand why kings, maddened by the

receipt of unwelcome news, would order the execution of the emissary. I wondered if this one had shared in ravishing the girl before she died.

But my anger was also turned inwards upon myself, for failing in my duty to punish a crime directed, if I had only known it, against me. How many others have died without my knowledge, while I have waited to surrender myself to my Furies? And how many more will suffer if I do not move now to protect them from the curse that has followed wherever I go?

Even for minor actions and decisions of which I am hardly aware, for something as seemingly inconsequential as an adjudication over a piece of land, innocent strangers are still paying the price.

This man, this squatter's son from Manáus whose face even now I can barely remember, chose to provoke me into retaliation by callously taking the life of a child. I am the carrier of a fatal disease to which I remain immune while others succumb simply through contact with me.

'Tell the man,' I said, 'that I will be there at dawn. And tell him I will be coming not to take him prisoner and hand him over to the Indians but to kill him myself.'

The messenger bowed. 'He will be pleased to hear it, Patróno. He says he has grown tired of waiting for you.'

As he turned to leave I called after him. 'As for you, I want you off my land tomorrow, and I never want to see your face on my estate again.'

He stiffened at that, but still the smirk clung to his lips. 'You may not be here to see, Patróno.'

'I will leave orders with Esquamillo that he is to shoot you on sight.'

At last the smile left his face.

He shook his head. 'You are old, Patróno. And this land is not yours. You have taken it from others. Just as others will take it from you. This is a land for the strong, not the weak.'

He left before I could answer him. Which is as well, for I would not have found the words.

He was right.

2

I dreamt last night that I was in the signal box. There was a woman fallen on the tracks. A young girl. The stream of faceless people moved past her without noticing. I could see that, in the distance, a train was approaching at great speed, its ugly stain of smoke filling the sky.

The girl lifted her face to me. It was Rachel's face.

She stood up, looking to see what I would do. I dare not wave to her, conscious of unseen eyes observing to see how I would react.

Slowly the girl turned. She started walking along the tracks towards the approaching train. I could hear the shriek of the whistle swelling in volume. I wanted to cry out, but my voice choked in my throat.

She began to run, hurrying to embrace the hurtling locomotive.

I left the signal box, racing after her. I did not care who was watching.

'Rachel!' I screamed. 'Rachel!'

But my voice was lost in the shriek of the engine.

This morning I went to Father Lorenzo, to seek confession.

He looked stunned. I could see his mind working, trying to understand why this had come about. He must have persuaded himself it was Ruth's influence. That she had accomplished what he, in all these years, has failed to achieve.

He was in his work clothes, polishing the mahogany altar rails. He wanted to change into his surplice, but I dissuaded him. I said I would prefer him to receive me not as a priest but as a friend. I warned him that I had a lot to tell and suggested the intimacy of his parlour, with its homely array of holy pictures, rather than the stark chapel where the old women drop in unexpectedly to mumble over their beads.

He pulled up a chair for me to sit beside him at his dining table. At my age, he said, it was unnecessary to kneel.

But I did.

I asked him to close the door so no one could look in on us.

And I knelt.

I told him everything, keeping my eyes closed, not wanting to be distracted by the expression on his face. I was on my knees for more than an hour, beginning to slump back on my heels, until he took me under the arm and gently lifted me into the vacant chair.

I will say this for him. He never interrupted. I heard him catch his breath now and then, but he uttered no word and asked no question.

At the end, when I had nothing left to offer, I opened my eyes and saw the tears in his.

He said it was not enough to grant me absolution. We must celebrate Mass together, there and then, just the two of us. He had waited so long for this. And I had waited too long for the blessed sacrament of communion.

I pointed out that I had come unprepared for communion, but he insisted that, in my heart, I had been preparing for it all these years.

I indulged him. He has been the friend to whom I have denied so much. I could not deprive him of this celebration. And I wanted the solace of that wafer between my lips. I wanted to believe that it was possible to be forgiven.

When the mass was over, he clasped my shoulders.

'Thank you, thank you,' he whispered. 'You cannot know how much I have wanted this.'

'And I, Father. And I.'

I could see something was troubling him. 'Is this,' he asked, 'because of your promise to the Indians? Has the time come to deliver yourself to their justice?'

'No, Father,' I replied. 'This is not yet the full year I asked. Not yet the rising of the thirteenth moon.'

He smiled, relieved, not knowing how I had lied to him, with the wafer of Christ still fresh in my mouth, by telling only part of the truth.

Two letters arrived in yesterday's mail, the second postmarked New York. The photographs have come out better than she expected. She is working on a paper she hopes to have published in the next few months. Already she is beginning to cast around for her next project.

How far have I got with my translation of the diary? she asks. When can we announce our discovery?

She doesn't even mention the topic of our conversation by the river. As if it never took place.

Aren't we lucky, she says, to live in a world where so much is possible? She wants me to seize the opportunities it provides. It is not too late. I still have the physical and mental agility of a much younger man.

I sniff the envelope to see if I can catch her scent. But it comes from another world. One that bears no relation to this. It carries nothing to me but her words.

Estancia moves silently about her business, but I see in her eyes that she has learned the gist of my conversation with the messenger, that she knows of the appointment I will keep at dawn tomorrow. She tries to convey to me that she does not want me to die, that she will be praying for my finger on the trigger.

My eyes tell her in return that I am grateful for her prayers.

She loves me, but she loves her tribe, and they have suffered so much for so long. God is not the only one who waits patiently for atonement.

Outside the day is waning. The sinking sun is casting its last ebb tide of light on the walls of a room that has given me so much pleasure. Soon all the sound will wash from the leaves, like the dying cadence of a musical chord.

She brings Eduardo to kiss me goodnight.

I try not to let the fullness of my love show in the way I hold him to me. I do not want him to look upon this as a leave-taking. He still asks for Ruth. When will we go climbing again?

I release him and he goes, and I turn my face away to seek this page of my journal, where I write these words to you, Rachel.

Beside the journal lies Ruth's pistol. And standing propped against the escritoire is Esquamillo's shotgun. Both are loaded and ready.

This afternoon Esquamillo and I crept away, while Estancia was bathing Eduardo, to the clearing in the forest. Esquamillo was determined he would improve my aim. He is distressed that I know so little about guns. The Smith & Wesson proved more accurate than I anticipated, but my draw is painfully slow.

When we returned to the house he brought to me, as he has always done, the tally from this morning's collection, together with the rosters for tomorrow, of tappers who would normally be up on their rounds long before I am awake.

I could not take in the names, or bring myself to sign the authorisation, seeing instead another list, with columns of faceless humanity on a cargo manifest.

Gently he placed the pen in my hand and steered my fingers to the dotted line, as if to remind me I am only doing what I have always done, that there will be other lists, other signatures. And tomorrow is, after all, only one more day.

I told him that if I do not return from my appointment – if I should fail in my mission – he is to organise a party to hunt the killer down. Looking into his eyes, I saw the instruction was unnecessary.

Returning to the list, I noted that the name of the man I have dismissed was not among them. Esquamillo assured me he has packed and left, mercifully without a family to uproot.

Tomorrow I will do my utmost to dispatch his accomplice before he kills me.

And if I succeed, I will still have bullets in the pistol for myself.

I am tempted to believe he has made the same provision. It is not inconceivable. I have read somewhere that those who kill without compunction are but the modern-day equivalent of the classic Malay *amok*, the killer who must kill in order to be killed. My death will perhaps release him from his need to go on living.

And the Furies can then claim both of us. For they too have waited long enough.

My good friend Lorenzo reminds me that Christ, when they nailed him to his broken tree, said, 'Forgive them, Father, for they know not what they do.'

I was one of them, Rachel.

I knew not what I did!

Forgive me.

A NOTE ON THE AUTHOR

Peter Moss was born in Allahabad, of Anglo-Indian parentage, in 1935, and spent his childhood in remote railway settlements in Bengal and Bihar. After National Service he resumed his career in journalism, working for the *Malay Mail* in Kuala Lumpur. In 1965 he joined the Government Information Services in Hong Kong, where he has remained ever since. *The Singing Tree* is his first novel.